# I Heard Good News Today

## Stories for Children

Cornelia Lehn

Library of Congress Catalog Card Number 83-80401
International Standard Book Number 0-87303-073-7
Printed in the United States of America
Copyright © 1983 by Faith and Life Press
718 Main Street, Newton, Kansas 67114

Illustrated by Ralph A. Schlegel
Design by John Hiebert

To my sisters,
Tina, Helen, and Sara

# Foreword

In a society where there is little evidence of strong Christian morality, stories for children emphasizing commendable examples of behavior have been increasingly difficult to find. It has been a challenge for adults to find good mission and service stories to tell to children. Some worthy stories could be found only in books no longer being published; other stories were only in the memories of persons and needed to be recorded in printed form. Because of repeated requests for stories of this kind, Women in Mission of the General Conference Mennonite Church commissioned Cornelia Lehn to write this book.

Cornelia is well known for her love of children and for her gifts as teacher, writer, and storyteller. Her previous books of stories, *God Keeps His Promise* and *Peace Be With You,* have been a valuable resource for the church.

We are grateful to Cornelia for recording in *I Heard Good News Today* the experiences of others in an interesting story-telling format. Teachers, parents, and pastors will enjoy sharing these stories with children in worship services, at home, in Sunday school, and in daily vacation Bible school. We believe the material will be inspiring both to children and to adults who read it.

We trust that this book will prove to be a useful tool in helping to spell out the nature of Christian discipleship and what it means to love, share, and care under the lordship of Jesus.

Lora S. Oyer
Women in Mission

# Preface

Jesus told his disciples, you will be my witnesses in Jerusalem, and in all Judea and Samaria, and to the ends of the earth" (Acts 1: 8 NIV).

The stories in this book, written for children, show how this word of Jesus became a reality throughout the centuries.

In the first story the good news is identified. Mary Magdalene is the first person to whom Jesus appeared, and the first person to bring the good news of his resurrection to others. From there on, in ever widening circles, the stories show how Gods messengers take the words about Jesus Christ from country to country, and how the people who hear it and accept it become Christ's followers.

It is my hope and prayer that the stories will help the boys and girls in our congregations grow up to be strong men and women of God who will again tell others about the Savior and spread the love of Christ wherever they go.

The stories were written primarily for telling. I hope that pastors will be able to use them in their sermons; that workers with children will find them helpful in Sunday school, in Summer Bible school, in intergenerational groups, in camp settings; and that parents will tell or read them during family story time, while driving long distances, or on vacations. Of course, I also hope that children will want to read them for themselves.

It was a fascinating adventure to trace the path that the good news has taken all over the world and a great privilege to become acquainted with the many people who, for the love of Christ , endured hardships and were even willing to die in order to speed it on its way.

The writing of this book was commissioned and funded by Women in Mission. I thank the Commission on Education for giving me a six months' leave of absence, and Edna Dyck for being willing to do my work during that time.

I am deeply grateful to the many friends who helped me to locate sources in libraries and who lent me their books; to returned missionaries, relief workers, and others who were willing to share their stories with me. Without them, this book would not have been possible. I would also like to thank Lois Deckert, Herta Funk, John Gaeddert, Gladys Goering, James Juhnke, Robert Kreider, Lora Oyer, Alyce Reimer, Mary Rempel, Blanche Spaulding, Mabel Suderman, and Joan Wiebe for reading the manuscript critically and for giving me helpful suggestions.

Acknowledgments and sources for the stories are given at the back of the book.

From Africa there comes the story, "Singing the Bible." In it the children in their play, dance to an old tune and sing,

"I have heard good news today!"

"Oh, who told you?"

"God's messenger!" That is what this book is all about and that is where the book gets its title.

*Cornelia Lehn*

# Table of Contents

# Stories
# from the Bible

# 1.
# *The Good News*
## *(Mary Magdalene)*
## A.D. 39

Mary Magdalene got up very early on that morning, the third day after Jesus was crucified. It was still dark. She could not sleep. Quietly she slipped out of the house and walked down the road to where Jesus was buried.

Her heart was broken with sadness. Jesus was dead. She knew that. Oh, if she could only see him again. If she could only talk to him and hear his voice. How could he be dead! Mary Magdalene walked faster. At least she wanted to see his grave.

Suddenly she stopped short. She could see the grave. Yes. But something was different. There had been a great big stone in front of the cave where they had put Jesus' body, and now the stone was rolled away from the entrance. She ran forward. The grave was empty!

Terrified, Mary Magdalene turned and ran back to the house where some of the disciples were staying.

"Peter," she cried. "Peter! Someone has taken Jesus out of the grave and carried him away."

Peter and another disciple jumped up and together with Mary Magdalene they ran back up the road to the grave. They looked in. It was true — the grave was empty.

What could this mean? The two disciples slowly went home. But Mary Magdalene stayed. She stood by the empty grave, weeping. She didn't know what to do.

Once more she looked into the grave to make sure that Jesus was really not there. Then her heart almost stopped. There in the grave sat two angels clothed in white.

"Why are you crying?" asked one of the angels.

"They have taken my Lord away," she sobbed, "and I don't know where they have put him."

With that Mary Magdalene turned away from the grave, and there stood Jesus! But at first she did not know who it was.

Jesus said to her, "Why are you crying? Who is it you are looking for?"

"If you took him away, sir, please tell me where you have laid him," said Mary Magdalene.

Jesus looked at her and said, "Mary!"

With that Mary Magdalene knew it was Jesus.

"Master, Master," she cried.

"Don't cling to me," said Jesus, "for I have not gone to be with my Father yet. But go to the others who love me and tell them that I will go to be with my Father, who is also your Father; I will go to be with God, who is also your God."

Mary Magdalene hardly knew what she was doing, she was so happy. Now her heart was wild with joy. She ran back down the road. When she saw the disciples in the distance, she shouted, "I have seen the Lord. He is alive. I have heard his voice. He is not dead. Do you hear? Jesus is alive! And he told me to tell you that his Father is also our Father. He has made all things well."

(Based on John 20:1-18)

## 2.
# *What Does It Mean?*
## *(Philip and the Ethiopian)*
## About A.D. 40

The palace of the queen of Ethiopia was in an uproar. An official who took care of all the queen's money and treasures was going on a long journey. The servants were running here and there, polishing the carriage, brushing the horses' manes and tails, packing up food and all the things that had to be taken along.

"Where is he going?" whispered one servant to another.

"To the city of Jerusalem in Judea. They have a strange god there, and he wants to go and pray to him," answered the other her servant.

"A strange god!" exclaimed the first servant. "I wonder if he will tell us something about him when he gets back?"

"I don't know," mumbled his friend, as he ran to the carriage to put another basket in for the trip.

In the meantime the great official, in splendid robes, was ushered in to see the queen in order to say good-bye.

"Now, tell me again," said the queen. "Why is it that you want to pray in Jerusalem when we have so many gods of our own?"

"They know about a very special God in Jerusalem," said the official. "When I was there a number of years ago on business, I bought a scroll in which the writer, Isaiah, tells about this God. He is supposed to be the only God. I want to find out more about him, because I really can't understand all it says in the scroll."

"Go in peace then," said the queen. "We will wait for your report when you get back."

Soon after that the high Ethiopian official set out for Jerusalem.

While his servant was driving the chariot, the man had a lot of time to read. He read on and on in the scroll of Isaiah, but it was very puzzling to him. He could hardly wait until he would get to Jerusalem. Surely there someone would explain everything to him.

Finally the Ethiopian arrived in Jerusalem.

He went to the temple.

He met some teachers of the law.

They told him, yes, indeed, God Jehovah was the only God. He must obey all of God's laws or else God would be very angry with him. They even gave him a list of all the laws. It was a very long scroll. The man from Ethiopia became more and more worried. How could he ever keep all those laws?

Finally he set out for home. He was afraid that when he would give his report to the queen and the people in Ethiopia, they would think he was bringing them very bad news.

The carriage rolled slowly forward on the dusty desert road from Jerusalem to Gaza. Once more the Ethiopian had pulled out his scroll written by Isaiah. He read". . . as a sheep led to the slaughter or a lamb before its shearer is dumb, so he opens not his mouth."

The Ethiopian sighed. Who was this "he" that Isaiah wrote about and what did it all mean?

"God of heaven and earth," the Ethiopian prayed, "I do not know how to speak to you, but would you please help me understand more about you?" Then he read that part again out loud.

At that moment the man from Ethiopia saw someone running toward him. He had the carriage stopped.

A man came to the carriage, looking curiously at his scroll. "Do you understand what you are reading?" asked the man.

"How can I understand it, unless someone explains it to me?" answered the Ethiopian. "Come into the chariot and sit with me. Can you tell me what it means?"

The man climbed into the chariot. "I am Philip," he said. "I shall be glad to help you if I can."

The Ethiopian showed him what he was reading.

Philip smiled and said, "I have good news for you. What you have just read tells about Jesus, the Son of God, who died for us as a lamb that is killed. He died to save us from our sins. God knew we could not keep all the laws, so Jesus kept them for us. He showed us that God loves everyone and that he wants us to love him too."

The Ethiopian's eyes began to sparkle. "You mean God loves me too?" he asked.

"Yes, of course," answered Philip. "God loves you and all the people in Ethiopia. In fact, he loves the people in the whole world He wants them all to come to him."

The Ethiopian and Philip talked for a long time. The Ethiopian wanted to know more and more about God and his Son, Jesus.

As the carriage rolled on, they came to a spot where there was some water beside the road.

"Look, here is water," said the Ethiopian. "Why shouldn't I be baptized? I love the Lord Jesus and want to belong to him."

They stopped the carriage and got out. There in the water Philip baptized the Ethiopian.

Then the Spirit of the Lord took Philip away. Although the Ethiopian did not see him again, his heart was full of rejoicing. When he got back to Ethiopia he had good news for the queen and all the people.

(Based on Acts 8:26-40)

3.

# God Loves Everyone
## (Peter and Cornelius)
## About A.D. 40

The Apostle Peter traveled around the country preaching the good news about Jesus wherever he went. Sometimes he needed to stay in the same place for several days in order to help people and to talk with them. One day he came to the town of Joppa where he met a man named Simon. To make a living, Simon tanned animal skins to make leather. He lived in a house close to the seashore. He was a very kind man and welcomed Peter into his home.

One day lunch was not quite ready yet and so Peter went up on the roof to pray. It was quiet there and he could be alone. While he was praying, he suddenly had a vision. He saw heaven opened and something like a large sheet was let down to earth by its four corners. This sheet contained all kinds of animals, reptiles, and birds. Peter heard a voice saying, "Get up, Peter. Kill and eat."

"Oh, no, Lord!" Peter answered. "How can I do that! They are unclean and we are not supposed to eat them!"

"Do not call anything unclean that God has made clean," said the voice.

This happened three times and then the sheet was taken back to heaven.

Peter was still wondering what the vision meant when three men came to the gate of Simon's house.

"Is Simon Peter staying at this house?" they called.

The Holy Spirit said to Peter, "Three men are looking for you. Go downstairs. They will want you to go with them. Now do not hesitate to do so, for I have sent them."

Peter went down and said to the men, "I'm the one you are looking for. Why have you come?"

"We have come from Cornelius, the centurion," they said. "He is a righteous and Godfearing man, who is respected by all the Jewish people. An angel told him to have you come to his house so that he could hear what you have to say."

Peter invited the men into the house, and the next day they, together with some of Peter's friends, started on their trip to Caesarea where the Roman soldier, Cornelius, lived.

Cornelius had already invited his close friends and relatives. They were all sitting there ready to listen when Peter arrived.

"You know very well that it is against our law for a Jew like me to visit someone who is not a Jew," said Peter to the group of people. "But God has shown me through a vision that I should not call anyone unclean, and that I should go to your house. May I ask why you sent for me?"

Cornelius answered. He said, "Four days ago I was in my house praying. Suddenly a man in shining clothes stood before me and said, 'Cornelius, God has heard your prayers and remembered your gifts to the poor. Send to Joppa for Simon who is called Peter. He is guest in the home of Simon the tanner, who lives by the sea.' So I sent for you immediately, and it was good of you to come. Now we are all in the presence of God to listen to everything the Lord has commanded you to tell us."

Peter was deeply moved. How carefully God had prepared both him and Cornelius for this meeting! He had even told Cornelius exactly where he, Peter, was staying.

"Now I know for sure that God has no favorites," said Peter. "He accepts people from every nation who fear him and do what is right. God has told us this good news of peace through Jesus Christ, who is Lord of all, and the good news is for everybody."

Then Peter told the people in Cornelius's house all about Jesus.

He told them how Jesus had walked across the country doing good and healing the sick.

He told them how he had taught about God's kingdom.

He told them how he had been killed and raised by God from the dead. He also told them that Jesus had told his disciples to preach the good news of God's love to everyone.

"He is the one whom God chose to judge the living and the dead," he said. "Everyone who believes in him receives forgiveness of sins through his name."

While Peter was still speaking, the Holy Spirit came on all who heard the message. They began speaking in tongues and praising God.

Peter and those who had come with him were amazed. Peter knew now that these people were ready to belong to the church of Jesus Christ, so he baptized them.

Then Cornelius asked Peter and his companions to stay at his house for several days. They all had a good time together.

(Based on Acts 10:1-48)

# 4.
# *The Meeting at the River*
## *(Paul and Lydia)*
## About A.D. 45

Lydia was a good businesswoman. She had come from the city of Thyatira to open a shop in a city of Macedonia called Philippi. In her shop Lydia sold beautiful purple cloth. The cloth was very special. People liked to buy it.

Lydia enjoyed working in her shop, but she was not quite happy. Lovely clothes and other beautiful things were not the most important things in her life. To her the most important thing was to love God and do his commandments. She tried hard to do everything that God wanted her to do, but very often she did things that were not kind, things that were wrong. Then she was afraid of God. Would God punish her?

On the Sabbath, the day of rest, Lydia and some of her friends went down to the river to pray. It was nice and cool under the trees and nobody disturbed them there. It was the place where Lydia felt closest to God. When she heard the wind in the trees and the water rushing over the pebbles, she thought God must be very great and wise to make such a beautiful world. She wished she could learn to know him better, but there was no one to tell them very much about him.

One Sabbath day, Lydia and her friends were sitting in the grass beside the river. They were all thinking about God and praying silently when suddenly they heard footsteps.

Several men were coming down the path by the river. They were strangers. Lydia had never seen them in their meeting before. Who could they be?

"I am Paul," said one of the men," and this is Timothy. We have come to tell people about God and his Son, Jesus Christ. May we spend some time with you?"

"Oh, yes, yes," said Lydia eagerly. "We would like to know more about God. What is this you said about his son? I didn't know he had a son."

Paul started to tell them all about Jesus.

He told them that God loved everyone in the whole world.

He told them that he loved them so much that he sent his only Son so that all who believed in him could be saved from their wicked ways and live a life that lasts forever.

Lydia could not understand everything right away. She wanted to know more. So she kept on asking. This seemed exactly what she had been waiting for.

Paul and Timothy stayed in Philippi for a while, so Lydia had many opportunities to talk with them.

One day Lydia said to Paul, "Now I have accepted Jesus as my Savior. He has forgiven my sins. I have given my whole life to him and I know he as accepted me. I love him with all my heart and want to belong to him and his church."

It was a great day when Lydia and the people in her household were baptized. Now Lydia was no longer afraid of God. She loved God and this made her happy.

(Based on Acts 16:11-15)

# *Early Missionaries*

# 5.
# *I Will Go Where You Want Me to Go*
## *(Thomas)*
## About A.D. 39

The Apostle Thomas started. walking slower and slower. He kicked the dust up with his sandals. "Oh, I wish I didn't have to go to this meeting," he thought.

The apostles were coming together in Jerusalem to decide to which country each of them should go to tell the people about Jesus. They were going to pull straws.

Thomas wanted to tell people about Jesus. He was ready to go to some country to do it. But Thomas was afraid that if they pulled straws he would have to go where he did not want to go.

Even though Thomas walked very slowly, he finally got to the house where they were having the meeting. The other apostles were all there.

They all sat down together. After praying together they pulled straws. The Apostle Thomas was to go to India.

"Oh, no!" he cried. "It is just as I feared. India! It is impossible. I cannot go to India. India is too far away. No one knows very much about it, and, besides, I am Hebrew. The people there won't understand what I am saying. They might even kill me. No, I just won't go!"

Thomas stormed out of the room, a very unhappy man.

That night, however, when Thomas finally fell asleep, Jesus appeared to him and said, "Don't be afraid, Thomas. Go to India and tell the people about me. I will be with you every step of the way."

Thomas awoke. He knew Jesus had spoken to him. Jesus, whom he loved dearly, wanted him to go to India. And Jesus would go with him. Thomas said in his heart, "I will go wherever you want me to go, Lord Jesus. Your will be done."

The very next morning Thomas went to the marketplace to see what he could find out about going to India. He was sure to find people there from many lands.

As Thomas was walking around, looking this way and that, he suddenly came across a merchant who looked as if he had come from a foreign country.

"What is your name and where are you from?" asked Thomas.

"My name is Abbanes," said the man. "I have just come from India. King Gundaphoros wants me to bring a carpenter from here to work for him. Do you know of such a man?"

Thomas could hardly believe his ears. "I am a carpenter," he stuttered.

"What kind of carpentry do you do?" asked Abbanes.

"Oh, I work in wood, make plows and yokes and boats. I also work with stone slabs and have some experience in building palaces."

"You are my man!" cried Abbanes. "Will you go to India with me?"

It almost seemed like another dream to Thomas. Before he knew it, he was on the way to India.

It was a long, long trip in those days. Boats were slow. Thomas and Abbanes probably boarded a boat in one of the ports of the Red Sea and then sailed around Arabia and across the sea to South India.

Finally they arrived at the court of King Gundaphoros and Thomas started working for him.

Being a carpenter was not the most important thing to Thomas, however. Wherever he went, he was kind to the poor. He shared his food with the hungry and healed those who were sick. He learned the language of that part of India and told the people around him about Jesus. He founded many churches. Finally even King Gundaphoros became a Christian.

Many years went by. Thomas preached what he knew about God in many parts of India. Finally, another king, whose name was Misdeus, came to power. Misdeus was very angry when he found out that both his mother and son had become believers in Jesus. He planned to kill Thomas, but was afraid of the people because he knew they loved Thomas. So he led Thomas personally out of the city as if he were going to discuss something with him, and when they were away from the crowd he had several soldiers lead him away to be executed.

Thomas knew he was about to die. But now he was not afraid the way he had been years ago when he was first asked to go to India. On the way to his death, Thomas prayed, "My Lord and my God, you who have been my leader and guide wherever I have traveled, guide me now on my way to you. I have finished the work which you have given me to do.

Then Thomas was killed.

Not all ancient writings agree on the details of how Thomas got to India and how he died. But one thing is certain. When missionaries came to India many hundreds of years later, they found, to their surprise, people who called themselves *Thomas Christians.*

"Who brought the good news about Jesus to India?" the missionaries asked. "The Apostle Thomas did," they answered. "That is why we call ourselves by his name."

# 6.
# *A Job of His Own*
## *(John Mark)*
## About A.D. 45

John Mark loved the Apostle Peter. He liked his big booming laugh. He liked the way the Apostle Peter told the stories about Jesus.

John Mark was the Apostle Peter's helper. Wherever Peter went to preach the Word of God, John Mark went also. He did whatever needed to be done to make traveling and preaching easier for Peter. John Mark liked doing that, but sometimes he wondered whether God would ever ask him to do something on his own.

Many, many people came to hear Peter tell about what it had been like to be with Jesus. They listened spellbound as Peter told of the way Jesus had helped people, how he had died,

and how God had raised him from the dead.

They did not want to let Peter go because they were afraid they would forget something of what Peter had said. They wanted to memorize the words, but they were not written down anywhere.

One day the people took John Mark aside. "We know Peter is too busy to write down all the things Jesus did," they said. "You have heard him tell these stories many, many times. Please write them down and give the writings to us so we can read them over and over again and remember them."

John Mark thought about this request. The more he thought about it, the more excited he became. Maybe this is what God wanted him to do all by himself. He knew Peter's stories almost from memory. He could write them down just the way Peter spoke—short and to the point.

But John Mark wondered how Peter would feel about his writing down what really belonged to Peter. Maybe Peter would not like it. Maybe Peter would think it would not be quite the way it happened if someone else wrote the story.

John Mark decided to try writing the stories down before telling Peter. Every night when they were not on the road traveling, John Mark sat in his little room and wrote.

He was careful to say it just the way Peter had said it. He was careful not to leave anything out, and he tried not to make any mistakes.

He hoped Peter would not find out about his work until it was all done. But one night just as John Mark was almost finished, he heard the door open, and Peter came striding in. John Mark froze in his chair. He felt Peter bending over him and he knew Peter was starting to read what he had written.

"My son," said Peter finally, "I had a feeling something was going on. What is this that you are doing?"

Now John Mark told Peter everything—how the people had asked him to write the stories down so they could read them and remember them better, and how he was trying to write them exactly as Peter had told them.

Peter sat lost in thought. Then he said, "John Mark, I think this is a good thing. It is from the Lord. Many of the people who knew Jesus when he was here on earth have already died. I too might die soon. People must have some way of hearing the stories about Jesus accurately when we are gone. I know you are very thorough. There is no one on earth who can tell my stories as well as you can because you have been with me these many years. I thank you."

John Mark was happy. He finished writing the stories.

Later John Mark took his little book to Egypt and started a church there. After many years John Mark died, but the little book he had written went on being read. We have it in our Bibles as the Gospel of Mark.

7.

# Patrick Goes to Ireland
## (Saint Patrick)
## Around A.D. 400

In England around the year 400 there lived a very happy boy. His name was Patricius Sucatus, but for short he was called Sucat.

Sucat had parents who loved him and who were Christians. They had a lovely home. There were large fields and a wooded area where Sucat could play and do whatever he liked.

Often Sucat sat under a tree and dreamed about what he would do when he was grown up. Would he become a farmer? a hunter? or should he perhaps become a businessman?

But one day when Sucat was sixteen years old, something happened that changed his whole life. It started as a very ordinary day. Sucat told his mother and father after breakfast that he was going hunting in the woods behind their house. He took his bow and arrow and ran lightly down the trail into the forest.

All was quiet. He stopped and listened. He looked at the ground to see if he could find footprints of a deer.

Suddenly, someone from behind grabbed him. Sucat was a strong healthy boy, but he could not free himself. Several men held him as in a vise. Sucat did not know them. No matter how hard he struggled, they would not let him go.

The men were pirates from the east coast of Ireland who had come to England to look for boys whom they could sell as slaves.

Sucat could not even say good-bye to his parents. They did not know what had happened to him. The pirates bound Sucat's hands and dragged him off to their ship where they threw him into the dark hold below. Many other boys whom the pirates had stolen were there.

Sucat was dazed. He could not believe this had happened. One moment he was running around in the woods, a carefree boy, and the next he was to be sold as a slave.

When the ship reached Ireland, the boys, all chained together, were yanked off the ship and dragged ashore. There they were taken to a slave market.

It did not take long until an Irish chieftain bought Sucat.

"What is your name?" he growled roughly.

"Patricius Sucatus," said the boy proudly.

"Well, from now on your name is Patrick," said the man, "and you will tend my pigs."

So Patrick took care of his masters pigs. There was nothing else he could do. Often as he walked back and forth taking feed and water to them he thought, "Is this what I will do all my life?" He was very homesick for his parents and the life he had left behind.

One day a big storm came up. Thunder rolled across the sky and the lightning zigzagged everywhere. As Patrick was watching the beautiful sight, to his amazement he saw the other servants, who were Irish, huddled together with a look of terror on their faces.

"What is the matter?" asked Patrick.

"The storm shows that the gods are angry with us," whispered one of the men. "We must not have honored them enough. They might kill us!"

"Your gods are angry?" asked Patrick surprised.

"Yes," said another. "The priest tells us we have not brought enough food as offering. We brought all we could—our children don't have enough to eat as it is. But if the gods will only spare us today, we will bring all we have."

"But, but," stuttered Patrick, "the God I know is kind and good."

"Not our gods," said another of the men. "They don't care what happens to us. I hate them, but I have to do as the priest says or else I don't know what the gods will do to my family. They might all die."

The storm was slowly moving away, and Patrick had to look after the pigs so he could not stay to talk. But that night he lay awake and really thought about God—the God he had learned to know at home—the God who had made heaven and earth. The only God. The God who loved the whole world so much that he sent his own Son to earth to show people what he was like.

Suddenly Patrick realized how different the God he knew was from the gods the people around him believed in. He thought of Jesus, God's Son, who had compassion with people and who healed the sick and fed the hungry. He thought of Jesus who had loved everybody so much that he was willing to die for them. Patrick felt as if Jesus' love suddenly surrounded him in such a real way that from then on he talked to Jesus as his friend. He learned to love Jesus more and more.

As he learned to know Jesus, Patrick was also more concerned about the people around him. He talked with the other servants. He became friends with them and with his other neighbors. Now when he saw how afraid they were of their gods he wished with all his heart that they could learn to know Jesus.

Patrick began dreaming about how he could tell the people in Ireland about Jesus. But he was a slave. He could not move about as he wished. And he also needed to learn a lot more about

God and about his Son himself. He longed to study the Bible. How could this ever happen? It seemed impossible that it ever would.

Six years went by. Finally one night Patrick had a perfect chance to escape. His master was not at home and no one was watching. Why not try? At least he could try to get back to his parents. And then, who knows, he might be able to go back to school.

Patrick hurriedly grabbed his jacket and ran out of the house. He walked and walked. When morning dawned he saw the harbor. A ship was in the harbor with its sails up ready to leave.

Patrick ran as fast as he could. Gasping for breath, he finally reached the ship and found out it was leaving for England.

"Please take me on board," he begged the cap-tain. "My parents will pay you when I get home."

That is how it happened. Patrick came home at last and was reunited with his parents.

However, Patrick did not forget his friends in Ireland. He did not forget his dream of telling them about the God of love and compassion. Now he knew what he wanted to do with his life. He went to school to study the Bible and after several years he went to Ireland as a missionary.

Patrick stayed in Ireland all the rest of his life, and when he died many people believed in Christ. The Irish people loved Patrick so much that to this day throughout the whole world they honor him when they celebrate Saint Patrick's Day on March 17.

# 8.
# *How the Good News Came to Scotland*
## *(Columba)*
## A.D. 521

Columba was born in the year 521 in Donegal, Ireland. His father was king and had become a Christian because of the work Patrick had done in his country.

Columba liked to sit on his father's lap in the twilight and hear him tell stories. One of the stories Columba liked best was the story of how Patrick came to Ireland. His father had to tell it to him over and over again. Columba knew every word: First Patrick was dragged to Ireland as a slave. He herded his master's pigs. Then Patrick escaped.

Columba felt warm and good all over when his father said, "But Patrick knew we needed him. He came back to Ireland to tell us of the love of God and his Son, Jesus."

When the story was over, Columba sighed. Some day when he was grown up, he wanted to be like Patrick and tell others about Jesus.

But Columba had to learn many things before he could become a missionary. First, he had to go to school. That was a difficult matter. There were very few schools in Ireland. Columba had to go a long way from home to a place where there was a school. He was very homesick for his father and mother, but he loved his teacher, a good, kind, and very wise man.

All during his school years Columba never forgot that some day he wanted to become a missionary. He knew he needed to learn to read the Bible in order to tell others what was in it. But something puzzled him. Why did he have to learn to do so many other things?

In the school where he went, the students not only learned to read and write. They also had to learn how to grow vegetables, to build boats, and even to build houses. Columba did not know how that would help him to be a missionary.

Finally Columba grew up to be a tall, strong man. He became a preacher and a teacher first of all. He traveled all over Ireland to teach people about the love of Christ. He started schools where boys and girls could learn about him. He liked doing this, but he could never forget the stories about Patrick who had come to Ireland when the people there had never heard about Christ.

Columba knew that across the sea in Scotland lived many people who had still never heard the stories about Jesus. Who would bring the good news of his love to them? Should he? Did God want him to do it?

Columba had a hard time making up his mind. Travel was very slow. Columba knew that if he decided to go to Scotland as a missionary he would probably never see home again. He thought, "I will wait till next year."

The next year he thought, "I will wait another year. There is still enough time." Many years went by and Columba had still not gone to Scotland.

Finally when Columba was forty-two years old, he knew he must go right away if he was ever to go at all. Columba and twelve other men said good-bye to their families and to their country. They started out in a small boat to cross the stormy sea

Slowly the green hills of Ireland disappeared. They could see only the endless ocean and the huge sky overhead. Would they ever reach land?

The little boat bobbed up and down and the storm tossed it back and forth, but finally they saw land. They came to the Island of Iona off the west coast of Scotland.

Here on this island Columba and his helpers built themselves little huts and a church. They made a garden to grow food. They built boats to go to the mainland of Scotland to tell the people there about Christ. Columba needed everything that he had learned when he was in school.

At last Columba was where he knew God wanted him to be. For thirty-two years Columba traveled all over Scotland to tell the people about Jesus just like Patrick had done in Ireland. He started many churches and schools. He taught the people how to be obedient to Christ not just on Sunday, but every day of the week. Columba believed that all of life belongs to God.

Today the community on the Island of Iona is still flourishing. It is a part of the Presbyterian Church of Scotland. People still go there to learn to do useful work and to bring others to Christ.

# 9.
# *No Turning Back*
## *(Augustine)*
## A.D. 540 - 604

A long, long time ago there was a pope in Rome called Gregory I. He was the leader of the Christian churches.

One day as Gregory was walking around in the marketplace he came by the slave market.

He stopped short. He could not believe his eyes. A group of boys stood there ready to be sold. That was not so unusual in those days, but their hair—their hair was fair, like gold. And as Gregory stepped up to them, he saw their eyes were as blue as the sky. The people Gregory had seen so far all had brown hair and brown eyes.

"Who are these boys?" Gregory asked some of the bystanders.

"They are Angles from England," someone said.

"Angles!" exclaimed Gregory. "They look more like angels to me!"

Gregory knew that these beautiful boys from faraway England were being sold as slaves, and that they and their parents had never heard of the love of Christ. It made him very sad. Right then and there he decided that the Christian Church must send missionaries to England. He chose a man called Augustine to head up the project.

Augustine and forty other men started out for England. The trip was long and dangerous. They traveled for hundreds of miles. It was hard to ride through the forest when there was so much underbrush. It was even harder to ride up and down the rugged mountains. Sometimes they became very discouraged.

One day they met some people on the road. The people asked, "Where are you going?"

Augustine said, "We are going to England to tell the people there about Jesus."

The people could hardly believe their ears

"What! You are going to England?" they exclaimed. "You must be mad. Like as not the wild barbarians who live there will kill you all immediately. If they don't, you will certainly not convert them with the kind and loving words of Christ."

Augustine and his friends looked at each other. They were already very tired, and now this! What should they do? Augustine knew his friends did not want to go on.

Slowly Augustine said, "I will go back to Rome alone and beg Gregory to let us all come home."

Back over all those many miles traveled Augustine with a heavy heart. When he finally got to Rome, Gregory listened to him carefully, but then he said, "Augustine, it will not do to turn back. I cannot forget those blue eyed boys in the marketplace. The people in England must hear the good news that Christ loves them."

There was no choice. Augustine struggled back through the forests, up and down the mountains, and through the valleys. The traveling got even worse, but something happened to Augustine while he was traveling alone. He listened to God, and suddenly he was no longer afraid. He knew God was with him.

When he came back to the men who were waiting for him, he said, "We will go on. God is going with us. I don't know how the people in England will treat us, but I am sure now that we will have a chance to tell them about Christ and his love for them." On they went. When they finally reached England, they sent a messenger to King Ethelbert. What would the king do? Would he try to kill them as the people on the way had said?

The messenger came back. "King Ethelbert listened to your message," he said. "His wife is a Christian, so he has invited you to stay on the island."

Augustine and his friends collapsed with relief. Finally they could rest and prepare for their work.

Several days later, King Ethelbert himself came to see Augustine and his fellow missionaries. He did not come very close, however, because he was afraid that these strange men might practice some magic on him. He had heard that Augustine could make tails grow on those who irritated him! So he sat in the middle of an open field. Then he commanded Augustine to tell what he had to say.

The moment had come. Augustine told King Ethelbert the story of how God had created the world and all that is in it. He told him how God had sent his only Son, Jesus Christ, to save people from their sins.

King Ethelbert listened carefully, but then he said, "That is very interesting, but I shall stay with the religion my nation and I have believed in for so long. You may stay here, however, and tell the people about your God."

Now Augustine and his friends started preaching about God in the town of Canterbury. They lived among the people. They helped them and brought them the love of Christ. Many were converted and joined the little church in that town.

When King Ethelbert saw how Augustine and his followers lived, he became more and more interested in Christianity and started listening to what they were saying. In time he, too, became a Christian and was baptized. The queen was happy. She had hoped and prayed for this for years.

The good news about Jesus had at last come to the land of the fair-haired, blue-eyed boys whom Pope Gregory had seen in the marketplace. Many, many people became followers of Christ.

In 601 Pope Gregory made Augustine the archbishop of Canterbury.

Canterbury is still the place where the head of the Church of England lives. He is still called the *archbishop of Canterbury,* just as Augustine was so many years ago.

## 10.
# *The Tree That Points to Heaven*
*(Boniface)*
A.D. 724

It was Christmas Eve in the year 724. The moon shone brightly on the snow-covered trees and scattered a million diamonds on their branches. Through the beautiful whiteness walked a group of men. The leader, Boniface, walked first. He made tracks in the deep snow, and the other men, one by one in single file, walked in his footsteps. They had come to Germany as missionaries.

"Isn't it time to make camp for the night?" asked one of the men. They all stopped to catch their breath.

"No," said Boniface. "We have important work to do tonight. It is Yuletide. The people of the forest will already have gathered at the great oak tree to worship their god, Thor. They will make a sacrifice. We must get there to break the evil power their god has over them."

The little group of men hurried on through the snow. Finally they saw a red glow. A fire had been started in front of a huge oak tree. As they came closer, they could see a big crowd of people sitting in a half-circle around the fire. Their faces were turned toward the thunderoak, the tree sacred to the worship of their god. All the people were dressed in pure white. Something very special was going to happen.

Boniface and his men crept closer.

In front of the people stood a priest in a long robe. The priest lifted his arms. "This is the night when the sun dies," he chanted. "It is the hour of darkness. Thor, the god of thunder and war, who dwells in this oak tree, has shown us that he is angry with us.

"Our crops have failed. The wolves have devoured our sheep. Our enemies have defeated us in battle. We must once again feed the roots of Thor's holy tree with blood."

A murmur of approval ran through the masses of people.

The priest lifted his face and cried, "Thor demands that you give him the best and dearest that you have."

He walked over to the place where the children were watching the fire. He laid his hands on the head of the little Asulf, the son of the chieftain. The little fair-haired boy with the merry laugh was especially loved by the whole tribe.

"This is the chosen one," said the priest. "He alone can take away your sin."

Asulf's father and mother were frozen with horror, and a sigh went through the whole assembly as the priest led little Prince Asulf to a big stone in front of the fire.

Boniface and his men were standing behind some trees, watching. Noiselessly Boniface moved closer. The priest asked the little boy to kneel on the stone. Then he swung high the hammer of the god Thor.

But just as the hammer was about to comedown on the little boy's head, Boniface grabbed it from behind.

"No," shouted Boniface. "No! This sacrifice is not necessary. The God of heaven and earth is not angry with you. He loves you and sent his own Son to die for you."

The people jumped up. Some were angry and wanted to kill Boniface for interrupting the sacrifice. Others were overjoyed that their little prince was safe.

The chieftain stopped the noise. "What word do you have for us from the God of whom you speak?" he asked Boniface.

Boniface stepped forward. "The word is love, said Boniface. "Jesus, God's Son was born this night to be the Savior of the whole world. The power of evil is broken. Thor has no power."

Boniface pointed to the great oak tree. "You say this is Thor's tree," he said. "See if he will protect it."

Boniface motioned to his helpers. Quickly they came forward with their axes. They all went to work chopping away at the old oak tree.

The people were frightened. The priest muttered angrily. Surely the mighty god Thor would strike these men dead for cutting down his tree.

But nothing of the kind happened. All was quiet in the forest except for the noise the axes made. Finally the mighty tree crashed to the ground.

"Your god is dead," cried Boniface. "The true God bids you worship him and him alone."

Boniface walked over to a little fir tree standing near by. "Let this little tree which always remains green and points to heaven, remind you of the life Jesus has brought," he said.

Boniface cut down the little fir tree and carried it to the chieftain's hall. Little Asulf and his parents as well as the other people all gathered there and rejoiced in the good news Boniface had brought them about God.

The time came when the people in every home in Germany gathered around a fir tree at Christmastime to celebrate the birth of the Christ child and God's everlasting love.

# The Good News
## in Europe

# 11.
# *The Gospels of Lindesfarne*
## Around A.D. 700

People living on the east coast of England were never sure during the years around 700 when the Viking people from the north would swoop down on them with their terrible battle cries.

Their swift dragonboats came quietly. No one heard them before they were there. Then fire and death and terror descended upon a peaceful community. How everyone feared and dreaded the Vikings!

The monks living on the beautiful Island of Lindesfarne knew that someday they might be attacked by the Vikings also. They, too, feared them, but it was for a special reason. They had a very precious book that they did not want to lose. It was a book that contained the four Gospels.

Before his death Eadfrith, their beloved bishop, had copied the Latin words on carefully prepared animal skins called vellum. Patiently, word for word, he had copied them so that the words of Jesus would not be lost.

Eadfrith had hoped and dreamed that someday people would lay down their swords and spears and follow Jesus, whose banner is love. How could that happen unless the words of Jesus, who alone could save the world from its sorrow, were taken to everyone?

The book was very beautiful. Eadfrith, who was an artist, had decorated many of the capital letters with lovely flowers and pictures of angels. He had painted them in many colors. After Eadfrith's death a cover was made for the pages and a skilled smith had adorned it with gold and silver and precious stones.

This was the treasure that the monks were worried about. What would they do if the Vikings suddenly came? How would they save the book with its precious message of love and peace?

Then one day it happened. Someone saw the dragonboats approaching. Soon their beloved home would be in flames. They must act swiftly.

One of the monks ran to where the book was kept. He wrapped it carefully, and held it safely in his arms. Secretly the monks slipped down to where their boat was anchored. Under cover of night they rowed across the water to the shores of the English mainland.

Even in England, however, there was no safe place for their treasure. The Vikings came there also, and so the monks decided to go to Ireland.

On the way to Ireland, a frightful storm arose. The wind and the waves tore at their little ship. The monks struggled for their lives. Suddenly a towering wave came crashing down on them, and before their very eyes it washed their precious book into the angry water.

Their boat was driven back to England, and the monks barely escaped with their lives. They stood on the shore and looked into the foaming waves. Their treasure was gone. After all their careful planning and all their efforts, they had lost it.

Finally the storm died down. The sea was quiet again. When the tide was low, the people of the village nearby came down to the seashore to search among the rocks for anything of value that might have been washed ashore by the storm. The monks came too. Halfheartedly they looked here and there. They did not really believe that they would find the book, but they were so heartsick that they could not do anything else.

Suddenly one of the monks started forward. There, wedged between two stones, was that not a bundle? No, surely not! Probably some rags. With beating hearts they ran toward it. It was the book! With shouts of joy they opened the bundle.

"All praise to God!" whispered the monks.

"Our Gospels are safe."

"And not even damaged!" murmured one. "See, only a few sheets have become wet."

Once more carrying their precious book, the monks wandered homeless across the land. Finally one day they came to the monastery in the town of Chester-le-street and found a refuge for themselves and their treasure.

The Anglo-Saxon monks of that place looked with awe on the beautiful book, but few of them knew Latin. They wanted to read what was in this book, but they could not understand the language.

One of them, called Aldred, noticed something. The lines in the beautiful book were far apart as Eadfrith had copied them. Could he not write the Anglo-Saxon translation in the space between the lines?

After much thought and prayer, the monks of Lindesfarne gave their consent and so Aldred went to work. Word by word, sentence after sentence, he wrote the message between the lines in his own Anglo-Saxon tongue. For how can swords be laid down, and spears be put away, unless all the people know Christ and his love? And how can they all know about Christ unless they can read the good news in their own language? Eadfrith would have been pleased with what Aldred did.

In a special place in London where the people of England keep their dearest treasures, you may even today see the ancient volume. Your eyes may rest upon the very words that Eadfrith and Aldred wrote, more than a thousand years ago, in the Gospels of Lindesfarne.

# 12.
# *Margaret Queen of Scotland*
## Around the year 1000

About five hundred years after Columba had told the people of Scotland about Christ something else happened that was very beautiful and that brought great changes to that country.

It did not start with something beautiful though. It started with a big storm. All night huge waves crashed against the rocks on the Fifeshire coast. At Dunfermline, the royal residence, King Malcolm wondered what was happening to the ships at sea.

In the morning a servant rushed in to tell the king that a ship had been blown off course and had landed in a sheltered bay nearby. The travelers were apparently a royal family from England.

King Malcolm and some servants hurried out to bring the weary people into the castle. There was a princess, her son Edgar, who was heir to the British throne, and two daughters, Christian and Margaret. Because of political turmoil, they had been on their way to Hungary when they were caught in the storm.

Princess Margaret was a tall, lovely girl. Most ancient writings say so much about the beauty of her character that they say little about the beauty of her appearance. King Malcolm immediately fell in love with her and wanted her to marry him.

At first Margaret did not want to become a queen. She had set her heart on entering a cloister and serving God through meditation and prayer. But after some time she changed her mind and in 1070 Margaret married Malcolm, the tempestuous monarch of Scotland.

One of the first things the young queen did was to make sure that her people could come to her at any time. There was a stone near the palace on which she often sat so that anyone in trouble could come to her for help.

It soon became the custom at Dunfermline that every morning the poor were invited into the royal hall. When they were seated, the king and queen entered. The king stood on one side and the queen on the other side as, together, they waited upon and served the people.

King Malcolm showered Margaret with riches, but she looked on nothing as her own. She used everything in the service of others and helped to start schools and churches and shelters for the sick and needy.

The young queen was so fresh and happy and charming that everyone was drawn to her. The clergy as well as the chiefs of the clans accepted the reforms she suggested for the life of the church and state. She was wise and good and so they trusted her. More than that—they all loved her.

King Malcolm adored his wife. It is said that whatever pleased her, he loved for the love of her. He supported her in all that she did and realized that her strength came from God.

Margaret and Malcolm had eight children. Toward the end of their lives they lived in the Castle of Edinburgh. Here within the castle walls, Queen Margaret had a little chapel built where she could go and pray and be alone with God.

The little chapel still stands. You can see it there if you go to Edinburgh and climb up the hill to the great castle. You will find fresh flowers on the altar no matter when you come. They are placed there every week by the Margarets of Scotland, who have banded together in a guild to honor the queen after whom they were named and who, in what she said and did, directed the people of Scotland to a better way of life.

# 13.
# *I Want to Read*
## Around 1700

Almost two hundred years ago there lived in a village in France a little boy called Louis Braille. His father was the village harnessmaker, so Louis spent much time playing in the harness shop. His bright blue eyes did not miss a thing.

One day when he was three years old, Louis decided that he would make a harness too. He took a little piece of leather and got a sharp awl from his father's workbench. He tried to punch a hole in the leather the way he had seen his father do it. But the leather was tough.

He tried and tried. Finally he bent over to see better. The awl slipped and pierced his eye!

His terrified scream brought his father with one leap over the workbench. His mother and sisters came running. Even the neighbors came out on their doorsteps.

Louis was quickly taken to a doctor, but the

doctor could not help. The infection from the injured eye spread to the other also and one day little Louis could see nothing at all. He was blind.

Louis could not understand what had happened to him. Where had all the things gone that he used to see? Forlornly he sat on a little bench near the fireplace. It was always dark.

His family tried to help him as much as possible. His mother put a little toy dog in his arms and guided his fingers over it so he would understand what it was. His father encouraged him to explore the harness shop with his hands. His brother and sisters constantly described things to him.

What Louis liked best was to hear his sister Catherine tell him stories. "How do you know so many stories, Catherine?" he asked her one day.

"Oh," said Catherine, "when I was little, Grandma Braille told me stories, and then when I went to school I read stories out of books."

"When I go to school, I'll read stories out of books, too, won't I?" asked Louis.

But little Louis could not read stories like the other children. He went to school, but even though he held the reader just like the other children were doing, he could not get the book to talk to him.

"Are there no books for blind children to read?" he asked his teacher.

"No," said his teacher sadly. "There are no books for blind children."

Louis put his head down on his desk and cried. To be able to read books was what he wanted most.

Louis was soon at the top of his class because he remembered everything the teacher said. He did all his arithmetic in his head. But he could not read and he could not write.

The time soon came when the other children went on to a higher school. Louis could not go because he was blind. Sadly he sat in the harness shop and braided tassels for the harnesses his father made.

One day the pastor of his church came to their home. "I have heard of a school for the blind in Paris," he said.

Louis jumped up. "Will there be books there that I can read?" he cried, all excited.

"I think so," said the pastor. "At least I heard that the students from the school read from books before the king and queen."

"When can I go?" asked Louis, turning to his parents. "I want to go right away."

Louis went to the school in Paris, and found books there for blind people to read. But there were very few. They were huge. Each letter was raised so that fingers could feel and identify them. It did not take Louis long to learn to read these books and he had them finished in no time at all. Again there were no books for him.

Louis was told he must learn to knit and make slippers and not worry about reading. He learned to make slippers quickly, but he still wanted to read.

"Surely there must be some way for the blind to read and write," thought Louis to himself. If only he could discover it.

Louis resolved that he would find a way. From then on he spent every spare minute trying to think up an alphabet code that would cut down on space and that could be read quickly with the fingertips.

One day he was standing in his pastors study and feeling with his hands the many, many books on the shelves.

"Will I never, never be able to read books like these myself?" he asked the pastor. "Will I always have to depend on someone else to read to me?"

"Only God knows that, my son," said the pastor gently. "Trust him. I have a feeling that he has a special assignment for you."

God did have a special plan and a special assignment for Louis Braille. For several years Louis worked on an alphabet code. Sometimes he became very discouraged. Nothing seemed to work. But finally he got the idea of raised dots punched into the paper with a dull awl. He invented a way of organizing the dots in a six-location code so that every letter in the alphabet could be quickly punched and quickly felt by the fingertip.

At last he had done it! Louis copied his dot alphabet to take to the boys at school. One of them immediately took the alphabet code and punched a sentence. It said, "I can write." They were all jubilant.

That is how the Braille alphabet was invented.

# 14.
# *Who Is Guilty?*
## Nineteenth Century

The room in one of the courthouses in London was packed. The door opened and a small, very thin-looking man was brought in. His jacket seemed miles too big for him.

"Your name is William John Turnbright?" asked the judge.

"Yes, your Honor," answered the man in a barely audible whisper.

"Mr. Turnbright," continued the judge, "you stole a loaf of bread from one of the bakeries on City Road yesterday. Why did you do it?"

John Turnbright wiped drops of perspiration from his brow. "Your Honor," he said haltingly, "I have a sick wife and two children. They need food. I am unable to do heavy work and easier jobs are not available. Last summer I began to beg so that my family would not starve. This week, however, we had nothing left to eat. I did not know what else to do. I took the bread.

"I did not steal the bread, your Honor. I took it. There were so many loaves lying there. I wondered how many of them, when not sold, would be thrown into the waste containers as old bread. And only one of them would be enough to feed my family for one more day.

"I have an old Bible at home. I read in it sometimes when my wife and children are sleeping. It says there that those who have should give to those who do not have. Your Honor, how long must we wait until something is given to us?"

Exhausted, the man stopped talking. The judge who had been listening intently, was quiet for a while.

Then he said, "Mr. Turnbright, we have a law in this country that will not allow any exceptions. You are guilty of stealing and you must pay a fine of five pounds."

The judge paused. Then he pulled out his wallet and took out a five-pound note. He placed it into the container on his desk and said to the man in front of him, "This is your fine. It is paid."

Then the judge let his eyes roam over the people in the courtroom. "Besides the laws that are written into our lawbooks," he said slowly, "there is a universal moral law. According to that law we are all guilty. It is our fault that this man had to steal. Who wants to make restitution to him for that which we have left undone all these years? He who has ears to hear, will hear."

The judge took the container with the five-pound note from his desk and had it passed along the rows of people sitting in the courtroom. The container, filled to overflowing with money, was handed to Mr. Turnbright.

He held the container with both hands and stared down on it as if this were only a dream.

The court was dismissed.

# 15.
# *The Bible in Their Hearts*
## Around 1900

Karl Olsen sold Bibles. He didn't sell them in a store. Oh, no! He sold them trudging along the muddy roads from village to village in eastern Poland.

One day he was struggling along on a particularly bad road and he was tired. When he finally reached a village, he stopped at the first house.

A man answered his knock. From under his arms three children peeked out at the stranger.

"I am in search of a nights lodging, kind sir," said Karl. "I have money to pay for it and also a meal. I carry books to sell. I also read and tell stories to those in whose homes I stay."

At the mention of stories, the children looked delighted, and the man said, "Come in then out of the cold. My name is Antoni Kowalski. What is yours?"

"Karl Olsen," said the other.

Karl Olsen stepped into the house and met the whole family. There was Marja, Antoni's wife, who was cooking supper, and little Marja, Jan, and Baby Zosia.

The children wanted a story at once, but their father said firmly, "Let our guest get his hands warm before you pester him."

"And supper is almost ready," said his wife. "We shall eat first."

After supper the whole family gathered around Karl. He opened his pack and took out a Bible. "This is the most precious book in the world," he said. "Shall I read you a story from it? Here is a story Jesus told to the people who gathered around him."

Karl read the story of the good Samaritan. "You have been a good Samaritan to me," he said. "You have taken me in and given me shelter."

Then Karl told story after story. He told them about Joseph. He told them about David. He told them the story of Solomon and his beautiful temple. Little Marja sighed with pleasure as Karl finally closed the book.

"Let us buy a Bible so that Father can read from it every evening," she whispered.

"We are too poor for books," her father frowned.

"Please! Please!" begged little Marja. Finally her father gave in and bought the Bible.

Karl stayed with the family for two days. He made friends with others in the village, but no one else bought a Bible. Karl was disappointed. Sadly he trudged through the mud on his way to the next place.

Something very interesting was happening in the village he had left behind, however. Winter evenings are long in Poland. The sun sets early and after dark wolves roam the countryside. People stay indoors and there is nothing much to do.

On such evenings Antoni Kowalski and his family sat around the fire. Antoni would take down the Bible and read the stories Karl had marked. It was all new to them. They talked and wondered about what they had read.

Sometimes a neighbor would drop in. Antoni would reach for the Bible and say, "Listen to this teaching. Tell me what you think of it."

"Why should I forgive my enemy?" the neighbor would ask in astonishment. "Does it mean that I should chop wood for someone who has stolen part of my wheat crop? Surely, it cannot mean that!"

"Who knows?" Antoni would shake his head doubtfully. "A strange teaching."

Or they would talk about the verse, "Do unto others as you would have them do unto you." Little Marja and Jan listened as their father and mother discussed these things with the neighbor. Sometimes they remembered that when they were playing with other children they had not always been kind.

How the change came about no one could tell. Like yeast working silently in dough, God's Spirit was working in the hearts of people. The teachings of God's Word began to change Antoni and his family and his neighbors and their friends and the way they thought and talked and acted.

Then came the day when Antoni and his family decided to become followers of Jesus, not only in their hearts but openly. Others in the village wanted to belong to Christ too. Soon more and more came, and one day there were 200 Christians in this barren little village.

A number of years later, Karl Olsen was again trudging through the mud to that same village. He remembered that he had sold only one Bible here. He also remembered the family where he had stayed. He knocked at their door, scarcely thinking that they would recognize him.

Little Marja came to the door. She was taller than her mother now. She looked at Karl. Then she called, "Mama, Mama! It is Karl. He has come back!"

The family gathered around him. Word went flying through the village, and soon a big crowd was there to welcome him.

Karl was completely confused. What was the meaning of this? How did they happen to remember him?

Little by little the story came out. They showed him the Bible that was almost falling apart. They told him that over two hundred people had become followers of Jesus because of the message in it.

The next day they gathered for worship. During the service, Karl asked, "Is there someone here who has learned a verse and would like to recite it?"

For a moment there was silence. Then Antoni asked, "Verses or chapters?"

"Chapters!" exclaimed Karl. "Is there anyone here who knows a whole chapter of the Bible by heart?"

A little smile appeared on the faces of the grown-ups, and the children giggled.

"Yes," said Antoni. "You see, we were so afraid that we might somehow lose the only Bible we had that we started memorizing it. Each boy and girl, each man and woman was assigned a part, and now we can, as a group, recite most of the books of the Bible by heart."

Karl Olsen was stunned. He could hardly believe his ears. This time he stayed in the village a whole week, for these new Christians had many questions to ask him. And this time they bought all the Bibles and New Testaments and Gospels he had brought with him.

Karl thought in wonderment, "Many years ago I sold only one Bible here, and this is what has come of it! Truly, when God works in the hearts and minds of people, incredible things can happen."

With a light step and a happy heart, Karl Olsen went on to the next village.

# 16.
# *Little Tina*
## Around 1945

Little Tina lived with her mother and father in a Mennonite village in Russia.

One day when Tina was 3 1/2 years old, there was a terrible banging at their door. Men from the government came in and took Tina's father away. They would not say why or where they were taking him.

Not many weeks later, people in Tina's village were very frightened. There was a war and the enemy was coming nearer and nearer. They could hear the shooting.

One night a neighbor came to the house and said to Tina's mother, "Quick! Pack a suitcase and come. We are fleeing. The army is almost here!"

Frantically Mother snatched little Tina out of her sleep, dressed her, and threw the most necessary clothing into a suitcase. Quietly they slipped out of the house into the night.

A long line of silent people went trudging into the woods and on and on and on. They got tired and hungry and sleepy. During the night they walked, and during the day they tried to hide and find a place to sleep.

Finally they came to a country called Poland. The Polish officials did not like them either. They put all the women and children into a concentration camp where the mothers had to work hard in the fields. The overseers were very cruel to them and they had little to eat.

Little Tina cried and wanted to go home, but there was barbed wire fence all around them. They had to stay there.

One day the overseer called all the mothers down into the courtyard at noon and announced, "In fifteen minutes you are to bring all your children down here. We will take them away where they won't bother you in your work anymore. March!"

Tina's mother ran up the steps. She pressed little Tina desperately to her heart. Then with flying fingers she brought out a little bit of brown wrapping paper that she had saved, and a little stub of a pencil.

She wrote something on the paper, and then she said, "Tina, listen carefully to Mother. On this little piece of paper I have written your name, your birthdate, and my name. You must put it into your pocket and never, never lose it. You must not let anybody take it away, for if you do, Mother can never find you any more. And

now, Darling, don't be afraid. Even if Mother does not know where you are, God does. He will take care of you. Always pray to him, and some day he will bring you and me together again."

Then Tina had to go with all the other children. She bravely waved good-bye to her mother with one hand, and with the other she clutched a little bit of brown paper in the pocket of her ragged little dress.

When Mother could not see Tina anymore, she threw herself on her knees and begged God to watch over her little girl.

The children were taken a long way off on a train and then distributed among Polish people who were to take care of them.

A very kind couple took Tina into their home. They had always wanted a little girl. They hugged and kissed little Tina and gave her food to eat and put her to sleep in a clean little bed.

As the days went by, they loved Tina more and more, just as if she had been their own child. One thing puzzled them, however. One day the woman said to her husband, "What do you suppose our little girl is always hiding? During the day she never takes her hand out of the one pocket, and at night she hides something under her pillow?"

"Yes," said her husband, "it is strange. We must find out what it is."

But when they asked Tina, she would not answer them, and when they tried to pull her hand out of her pocket, she cried and screamed and ran out of their reach.

One night when Tina was fast asleep, they looked under her pillow. What should they see but a crumpled up bit of brown wrapping paper with Tina's name, her birthday, and her mother's name on it.

The man and his wife looked at each other. They were deeply touched.

"Her mother gave it to her for safekeeping so that she might know her again even if it takes years," whispered the woman.

Even though this couple had very much wanted to adopt Tina and keep her as their own, they decided then to give her up if Tina's mother should ever be found. They made sure that Tina kept the little bit of paper in a safe place.

At last after three years, Tina's mother was released from concentration camp, and she immediately went out to look for her little girl. She went to the place where it was rumored that the children had been taken and started asking from house to house. Tina's mother worried, Will I know Tina now that she is over six years old?

Will she know me? Has she kept the little piece of paper so that she can be identified?

Finally, Tina's mother came to the right place. Tina ran into her mother's arms. They knew each other, and the little piece of paper proved that they were mother and child. The kind Polish couple, who had taken care of Tina, were willing to give her up to be with her own mother again.

# 17.
# *God Can*
## (C. F. Klassen)
## Around 1946

A tall, handsome man walked briskly through the streets of a bombed-out city in Germany; he climbed over rubbish, he stumbled into holes, and every once in a while he stopped and looked more closely at parts of houses where people seemed to have found shelter.

Suddenly he bent forward in surprise and listened. Quite distinctly he could hear someone singing— it was the tune of a hymn that Mennonites used to sing in Russia.

The man quickly knocked at the door of the room from which the sound came. All was immediately quiet. Then someone slowly opened the door and a frightened face looked out.

"I am C.F. Klassen, a Mennonite from North America, and I am looking for my people," the tall man said in Low German.

"A Mennonite!" The people inside jumped up. They drew him into the room. They wept in unbelievable joy.

"You have come from America?"

"How did you know about us?"

"We were afraid that the Russians might find us here and take us back to Russia."

The people all talked at once.

"The Mennonites in North America are concerned about you. They want to help you. Do you know of any other Mennonite refugees around here?" asked C.F. Klassen.

That is how C.F. Klassen, sent by the Mennonite Central Committee, started to help Mennonites after the second world war. Soon he had to have helpers. Thousands of Mennonites who had lost their homes because of the war, came to refugee camps, waiting to be helped.

Again and again C.F. Klassen tried to persuade government officials to allow these homeless people to go to other countries. There were many difficulties, but always when things seemed impossible, C.F. Klassen would say, "We cannot solve this problem, but *God can.*"

And God did. More and more people were allowed to go to Paraguay, to Uruguay, to Canada, and to the United States. C.F. Klassen rejoiced with everyone that received permission to go and find a new home.

But he himself had no time to be at home. He had no time to rest. There was so much to do. One day he drove into Gronau, the place where thousands of refugees had come for help and where the camps were now empty. On that day God called him to his eternal home. C.F. Klassen could rest at last. His work was done.

# 18.
# *Too Much*
## Around 1950

For many years the boys and girls in Canada and the United States prepared Christmas bundles for refugee children. Often a Sunday school class together bought the things that went into it.

The bundle contained a dress if the package was meant for a girl, and shirt and pants if it was meant for a boy. In it were also a bar of soap and a washcloth. And always there was a toy.

All these articles were wrapped in a brightly-colored towel and pinned shut. Later the Mennonite Central Committee (MCC) added a New Testament in the language of the country where the package was going.

A whole pile of Christmas bundles was sent to Berlin after the second world war was over. The MCC workers were glad when they saw all the bundles that they could give away.

They called together the children in the area who had lost almost everything and had a Christmas program with them. An MCC worker told them the story of the little Christ child who was born in Bethlehem. They all sang German Christmas carols and prayed.

During the program the children had been looking at the brightly-colored towel-packages piled up on a table. They wondered what was in them. They could hardly wait until they could find out.

At the end of the program the MCC workers told them that boys and girls in North America had sent the bundles, and finally began distributing them.

Each child received a bundle. The children went wild with excitement and joy as they pulled out the dress or shirt and pants and smelled the soap, or as they began to play with the toys. They had never seen so many lovely new things in their lives.

The MCC workers watched the children enjoy their Christmas gifts.

But suddenly Harold Buller, one of the workers, became aware of a small boy standing in front of him. It was little Peter. He held out the Christmas bundle he had received and said, "It is too much for me!"

Harold looked at the little boy. He could not believe his ears. Peter was actually returning the Christmas bundle.

Quickly Harold squatted down so he could look into Peter's eyes. He put his hands on Peter's shoulders and said, "No, Peter. It is not too much for you. Do you know why?"

Peter shook his head.

"Because you can share it."

Peter looked at Harold. There was a light in his eyes and a smile crept over his thin little face. He clutched the Christmas bundle to his heart and ran away.

# 19.
# *The Miracle*
## *(Peter and Elfrieda Dyck)*
## 1947

During World War II , as in all the wars, there was death and sickness and poverty. Thousands of people became homeless and wandered around looking for food and shelter.

In some buildings in Berlin, over nine hundred Mennonite refugees from Russia had found shelter. Peter and Elfrieda Dyck, from the Mennonite Central Committee (MCC), had brought them there. But the people were very much afraid. They knew they might be sent back to Russia at any time if no home for them could be found.

Peter and Elfrieda, together with other MCC workers, were working hard to get them out of Berlin. They had chartered a ship, the *Volendam,* to take them and many other Mennonite refugees in Germany to Paraguay where they would be safe.

In order to get to the ship on time, the refugees in Berlin would need to leave by train on Sunday, January 26, 1947. Peter and Elfrieda were constantly working with the authorities to get permission to take the refugees out of the city through the Russian Zone to Bremerhaven. But they had not told the refugees yet about the ship in case it should not work out.

Saturday came, and still they did not have permission. The tension was terrible. Finally, in the evening, Peter was given definite word: the Russian leaders would not allow the refugees to travel through the Russian Zone.

Almost numb with grief, Peter and Elfrieda called the refugees together. They told them that a ship was ready and waiting for them at Bremerhaven, but that they could not go. Peter's voice broke. He had to leave for Bremerhaven to help load the ship and to tell them there that the *Volendam* would have to leave without the Berlin group.

The refugees sat with heads bowed down. They were silent. There seemed no hope for them. But then someone started praying. God, who had always been their help in time of trouble, surely knew about this hopeless situation. He could still help. They all prayed for a miracle. Then, quietly, they went out into the dark night to their respective houses.

But no miracle happened. Sunday and Monday dragged on into Tuesday and Wednesday and Thursday. They all knew that the *Volendam* would leave Bremerhaven on Friday.

On Thursday one of the refugees started packing a suitcase. The other men in his room watched him. Finally one of them asked, "What are you doing?"

"Just packing," he said. "We prayed for a miracle, did we not? I am getting ready. What if God really wants to answer our prayers, but we are not ready?"

At six o'clock on Thursday night, Elfrieda received a phone call that the refugees should be ready to leave in three hours. The permission to leave had been signed.

Quickly everyone got ready. Elfrieda arranged for twelve trucks to come and pick them up. She organized the people in groups so they could board quickly and without confusion. The trucks took the people to the railroad station through the dark streets of Berlin. No one stopped them.

Just before the train left, Peter Dyck came running to the station. He had just come back from Bremerhaven. They were holding the ship for another day! He jumped on the train and the long row of cars started moving slowly out of the station.

The people could hardly breathe, they were so excited. They were also frightened. What if the soldiers would stop them and send them back after all. Everyone prayed.

The train passed into the Russian Zone. It rattled through it and out of it again. Finally it came to Bremerhaven, and there was the *Volendam,* still waiting in the harbor for them.

# 20.
# *You Will Be Free*
## Around 1935

Far away in Siberia was a camp to which political prisoners as well as hardened criminals were condemned to hard labor.

Young Turkela from Finland was sent to this camp. He was a Christian.

The other inmates soon saw that there was something different about Turkela. He was open and friendly to everyone. Even when things got very rough, he still seemed to have hope.

Ivan, a violent criminal, was especially drawn to Turkela. Ivan was very bitter. Since his early childhood he had known nothing but rejection and injustice and hatred. Now suddenly here was someone in whom there was light and love and warmth. Slowly Ivan began to trust Turkela. They became friends.

During the long winter nights when snowstorms blew wildly around the camp, Turkela told his new friend about his faith in Jesus Christ. Ivan longed for love and meaning in life, but so far he could not overcome the darkness and suspicion that had been a part of him so long.

Turkela did not push him, but in response to the criminal's questions, he assured him over and over again, "You can experience it yourself. Christ can make you free from those things that enslave you. Ask him to free you. Try to obey his words. You will see that Christ has told us the truth. We can be free to live a new life."

After a long winter, spring came to Siberia. With it came a great deal of unrest in the camp. There was fighting between the inmates and the guards. Finally the prisoners revolted and refused to work.

The punishment was swift and horrible. Troops were sent to the camp. The inmates were lined up and every tenth one had to step up to be shot.

Turkela was standing right behind his friend. Quickly Turkela figured out while the counting was going on that Ivan would be number ten.

Only a few seconds remained. Turkela grabbed his friend's hand, whispered "You will be free," and exchanged places with him.

The next moment Turkela said loudly and clearly, "Ten!" and stepped forward.

Turkela was shot. But his faith now lived on in the friend for whom he had died. Ivan could no longer live without the Savior who had enabled Turkela to give his life for him.

# The Good News
## in India

## 21.
# Sit Down, Young Man!
*(William Carey)*
## 1761-1834

William Carey, who was born in England in 1761, was a most unlikely person to become a missionary.

Even as a little boy he was slight and frail. His family lived far away from any seaport so they did not hear about other countries. William had to quit school when he was twelve and was apprenticed to a shoemaker. He himself certainly did not dream of becoming a missionary. Why should he? No one in his church was going to a foreign country to tell others about Christ.

People in the Protestant church had forgotten that Jesus had told his followers to go into all the world and make all people his disciples. They had forgotten that someone had brought them the good news that Jesus loved them and that they should pass it on. And so William sat on his cobbler's bench, dreaming about all the things he would do when he was grown up, never thinking of being missionary.

William had always known about Christ. He had always gone to church. But the time came when Jesus became his own personal friend and Savior. Now William's life took a new direction. He wanted to do what Jesus wanted him to do.

When William read the Bible, he suddenly found out that Jesus had told his disciples to tell others about his love. William was shocked. If Jesus had said that, why was nobody doing it?

From then on William Carey dreamed of going to a faraway country where the people had never heard of Jesus and telling them of his love.

On the wall of his shop he tacked up a big map of the world. In the evenings he read far into the night. Soon he knew more about foreign countries and the people who lived there than anyone else in England.

He found out that there were slaves in many places in the world who were treated cruelly. He found out that they had never heard about Christ. William started praying for the slaves. But when he started praying for them he realized God wanted him to do something about their hard life.

One of the first things he did was refuse to buy sugar from the East Indies because the sugarcane was raised by slave labor. Another thing he did was to talk to people about spreading the good news of Christ's love to those who had never heard it. He stood up in a ministers' meeting and said, "Jesus gave his disciples the command to go into all the world and bring the good news of salvation to all people. Should we not obey that command now and bring the gospel to the heathen?"

The idea was completely new. They had never heard of such a thing. The chairman of the meeting frowned. "Sit down, young man," he snapped. "When it pleases God to convert the heathen, he will do it without your help or mine."

William sat down, but he knew he would stand up again some other day. He would not give up.

And he didn't. He spoke, he wrote, he preached.

"Expect great things from God," he cried, "and attempt great things for God.,"

Great things began to happen. The Baptist Missionary Society was founded. William Carey together with his wife and children went to India and started mission work there. He helped the poor, and made many economic reforms. He translated the Bible so the people could read it in their own language. He preached, and started churches.

When people heard what William Carey was doing and saw the many hardships and disappointments that he had to endure, they wanted to help him. Many went to other countries also to tell people about Jesus. That is why William Carey is called the father of modern missions.

## 22.
# *Never, Never, Never!*
## *(Ida Scudder)*
## 1890

Ida Scudder, granddaughter of John Scudder I and daughter of John Scudder II, definitely had a mind of her own. Her grandfather had been a medical missionary in India. Her father and her six uncles were missionaries in India. Several of her cousins and brothers were preparing to be missionaries in India. Everybody was expecting her to do the same. But she was certainly not going to allow herself to be squeezed into the Scudder mold!

First of all, she was angry with her father and mother for leaving her in America to go to school when they went back to India after a furlough.

Secondly she hated the poverty of India—the hot crowded streets, the smells, the beggars. Most of all she hated to think of the children starving to death. She did not want to see that again. She would stay in America where she could enjoy clean air, uncluttered streets, and a comfortable home.

Right now, in 1890, Ida was having a great time at school with her friends. She was beautiful and popular. She dreamed of a future holding only fun with friends, wealth, and adventure.

Then, one day, a cable came from her father in India. It said, "Come immediately. Your mother ill and needs you."

Ida was stunned. She wanted to see her mother again. She had missed her terribly and she wanted to help her. But go to India? Never, never, never!

That night Ida tossed and turned until morning came. What should she do? Finally she saw a way out. She would go to India, but she would only stay until her mother was well again. Then she would come back to America and plan her life the way she pleased.

Ida Scudder returned to India—to the dust and dirt and poverty and starvation she remembered. She was glad to be back with her parents and she helped them with their work as much as she could. But always she dreamed of the time when her mother would be stronger and when she could go back to America.

One night when her mother was already asleep and her father was still working in his study, Ida was writing a letter to a friend back at school. All was quiet. Suddenly she heard something. Were there soft footsteps on the verandah or was she just imagining it? She felt as if someone was peering at her through the darkness. And then she heard it very clearly— a cough in front of her door.

Ida was relieved. She knew that in India a cough is the same as a knock. She took a lamp and went to open the door.

There on the verandah stood a young Hindu man.

"What is it?" asked Ida. "Can I do anything for you?"

"Oh, yes!" said the man anxiously. "I desperately need your help. My young wife, who is only fourteen, is dying in childbirth. I heard you had come from America and could help her. Please come!"

"I am sorry," said Ida sympathetically. "It is my father who is the doctor. He is right next door in his study. I will take you to him."

The young man was horrified. "You don't know what you are saying," he said. "In my religion no man other than a member of her own family may ever look at a woman."

Ida tried to persuade him to let her father come, but he only shook his head and finally asked sorrowfully, "Then you won't come?"

"It would do no good," cried Ida. "I don't know anything about medical care."

In despair the young Hindu turned away and walked down the steps into the night.

Ida went back to her letter writing, but she could not forget the fourteen-year-old girl who was dying. She could have helped her if she had been a doctor.

After a short time, she again heard footsteps on the verandah. She jumped up.

There in the door stood another man. "Salaam, Madam," he said. "May Allah give you peace. Will you help me?"

"Of course," said Ida. "What can I do for you?"

"I am afraid my wife is dying," he said, his face sad and troubled. "I heard there is a doctor here who has recently come from America."

Ida rushed to get her father. "Here is the doctor you are looking for," she said. "I'll come with him to help, if you want me to."

"Madam," said the man, "you don't under-stand. We are Muslims and in our faith only men of the immediate family may enter a woman's room. I came to ask you for help, not your father."

Ida watched the man walk slowly down the steps. Then she ran to her room and closed the door. She couldn't stand it anymore. She just wanted to get out of India where things like this could happen, and go back to America.

Before long she heard a voice outside. Oh, perhaps one of the men had changed his mind! Perhaps they could still save one of the women. Ida opened the door.

But the man standing there was neither the Hindu nor the Muslim. It was the father of one of the children Ida was teaching at the mission school. She knew his lovely wife with the dark smiling eyes. She was no older then Ida.

The man said, "Please come to my house. My wife is very sick. She will die if you don't come."

"I am not a doctor. It would not do any good if I should come," said Ida again. "Let me call my father. He is a doctor. He will help you."

Before he even opened his mouth, Ida knew what he was going to say. She could see the disappointment in his face. He could not let a man come. He wanted a woman.

"Won't you come?" he pleaded again.

It almost broke Ida's heart that she could not help. After this man too had gone, Ida slowly went back to her room. How could such a thing happen three times in one night? She wondered if God was trying to say something to her.

The next morning she heard that all three of the women had died during the night.

Once again Ida went to her room and closed the door. When she came out, she went to her mother and father and said, "I am going to study to be a doctor so I can help the women of India."

That is exactly what Ida Scudder, the missionary doctor, did for the rest of her life. She helped the women, but she helped the children and the men as well. In the town of Vellore she had a big hospital built. She also planned a Christian medical college there where men and women could study to be doctors. She created a leprosy rehabilitation center and a mental health hospital. All these buildings became the greatest medical center in all Asia.

Ida Scudder taught the people of India by her words and actions that God is love. She loved the people and the people loved her. Even when she was an old, old lady and came back to her beloved hospital to visit, the patients reached out their hands to her just to touch her and have her smile and speak to them.

When someone asked her, "Don't you feel a great satisfaction when you see this beautiful hospital and remember how it all started?"

"Yes," she said, her face radiant. "God has been very good to me."

After all those many years, Dr. Ida Scudder had no regrets that she had chosen the way she did when she was young. She had only thanksgiving.

# 23.
# *A Christian Holy Man*
## *(Sadhu Sundar Singh)*
## Around 1900

Almost a hundred years ago, a boy, whose name was Sundar Singh, was born in India. His parents were wealthy, so Sundar grew up in a lovely home. He had everything that a little boy could wish for.

Sundar's mother was gentle and kind. She was also very wise. She taught little Sundar that the beautiful home they had and all their belongings were not nearly as important as peace of mind, or inner happiness. She often went to the holy men called *sadhus* for advice. Little Sundar went with his mother wherever she went, for he was the youngest in the family. Often his mother would say to him, "Sundar, someday you must become a holy *sadhu.*"

Sundar did not doubt that someday that is what he would be.

Sundar loved his mother deeply and he was very sad when she died. He was only fourteen, but from that day on he searched for the peace of mind that had been so dear to his mother. He read all the sacred books of the Hindus and the Mohammedans. He memorized many passages. He went to see the priests. He talked to the *sad-*

*hus.* But nothing brought rest to his heart.

Sundar knew about the Christian religion, but he hated it because it taught things that were opposite from what he had learned in childhood. One night Christ appeared to him and said, "Why do you oppose me? I am your Savior. I died on the cross for you."

When Sundar saw the love in the face of Christ, all his opposition melted away. He knew he was forgiven and accepted. At that moment the peace he had searched for so long came into his heart. The struggle was over. With a heart brimming with joy, Sundar went to his father's room and said, "I am a Christian!"

Sundar's father did not take the statement seriously. He just told Sundar to go to bed. But when it became clear that Sundar had really decided to follow Christ and join the despised Christians, his family thought it was too horrible to believe.

At first Sundar's father pleaded with him tenderly. Surely he would not reject all his mother had believed. When he saw his father's tears, Sundar's heart almost broke, but he knew he must love Jesus more than his mother and his father.

His uncle took Sundar to the cellar of his large mansion. There he unlocked his safe and showed the boy more jewels and money than Sundar had ever dreamed existed. "All these shall be yours if you will remain with us," his uncle said. Sundar was dazzled, but when he thought of the love of Christ he found it easy to say no.

His brother-in-law, who had a high position, took Sundar to the *Raja* or king of that area. The *Raja* offered Sundar a great position in his service. But even the *Raja* could not change Sundar's deep devotion to Christ.

Sundar had successfully passed the first three tests. His family could not bribe him into rejecting Christ. Now they tried to frighten him.

"You are no longer a son of this house," said his father angrily. Sundar had to eat and sleep outside. His eyes filled with tears. He could hardly bear it.

Sundar's own brother was now his bitterest enemy. He called Sundar names. He was mean to him. He made fun of Jesus.

Finally, Sundar's father told him that before sunrise the following day, he must leave home. For the last time Sundar lay down on the verandah to sleep. Then, early in the morning, he left his beautiful home where he had been so happy. He went out into the world, homeless, friend-less, and with only the clothes he was wearing. He had left all to follow Christ.

What now? Where should he go and what should he do? Sundar knew he belonged with other Christians. So he went to the American Medical Mission at Sabathu where he was safe from persecution and where he could study the Bible.

On his sixteenth birthday Sundar was baptized as a Christian, and thirty-three days later he put on the simple orange robe of a *sadhu* or holy man.

Barefoot, with no earthly belongings except for the Bible under his arm, he set out as a Christian *sadhu* to evangelize India. The people were familiar with holy men. Sadhu Sundar Singh was able to reach those who would never have listened to a white missionary.

Sundar was often hungry and cold. On his travels many people made fun of him. At times he was beaten and tortured. But always Sundar went on with his work for Christ.

The time came when thousands of people thronged to hear Sadhu Sundar Singh preach. Even his father became a Christian and was reconciled to his son.

No one knows how Sadhu Sundar Singh died. He started on a long dangerous journey through the mountains to Tibet and was never heard of again.

## 24.
# He Who Loses His Life Will Save It
*(Sadhu Sundar Singh)*
## Around 1900

Sadhu Sundar Singh, the Christian holy man, traveled all over India to bring the good news of Jesus to all who would hear. He even went to Tibet where no white people were allowed.

The journey to Tibet was very dangerous. There were sharp jagged rocks and deep gorges.

He and his Tibetan friend climbed up to the slopes of everlasting snow, where the wind cut like the lash of a whip and the sun on the snow almost blinded the eyes.

Sundar and his companion were trying hard to reach a shelter before nightfall. If they didn't, they would freeze to death.

It was already growing dark when they saw something lying beside the trail. A mans hand was sticking out of the snow. His body was half buried in the drifts.

"Don't stop," said the Tibetan. "We must hurry on or else night will overtake us. The man is probably dead or at least too far gone to be helped."

"Go on, then," said Sundar as he bent over the man in the snow. The Tibetan continued walking along the trail as fast as he could.

Sundar laid his hand on the man's breast. The heart was still beating.

With a struggle, Sundar raised the man, and carrying him on his back, staggered on against the terrible wind. The snow was hard to walk in and his heart beat fast under the burden.

"Lord, give me strength," he prayed.

Finally he saw the shelter. The great effort of carrying the man had made Sundar warm all over. He and the man on his back reached safety. But there on the path before him lay his Tibetan companion frozen to death.

# 25.
# *Your Hands Will Do Their Work Again*
## *(Mary Verghese)*
## Around 1930

Mary Verghese, a young Christian girl in India, came to Dr. Ida Scudder's hospital in Vellore to train as a doctor. How thrilled she was when her first surgery was a success! She dreamed of helping many, many people. It soon became clear that she would be a great surgeon.

One day, the student doctors or interns were going on a picnic. They asked Dr. Mary Verghese to go with them. Among the group was a young student who had just received his driver's license and wanted to drive the car in which they were going.

For a long time he drove well. Then the car came up to a slow-moving bus. Each time the young driver tried to pass the bus, the bus driver pulled out and refused to allow him to pass. This made the young driver so angry that he lost his temper and passed anyway.

He swerved to miss a bridge. The car turned over and rolled down a steep embankment.

Everyone was seriously hurt. Dr. Mary was so terribly injured that they thought she was dead. All were brought back to the hospital.

Dr. Mary slowly regained consciousness, but her spine was so badly injured that she would never be able to walk again. Was this the end of all her dreams to help people? Mary Verghese decided it was not.

Through years of agony and pain, she trained herself to operate her own wheelchair, to dress herself, to move herself from her chair to her bed, to feed herself. Finally the day came when, from her wheelchair, she again performed a surgery. It was a success!

Dr. Mary said many times that she believed that God had saved her life for a purpose. She now knew what it was like to be helpless. But she also knew that if she did not give up it was possible to do some things by herself again.

She became especially interested in the leprosy patients at Vellore Medical Centre who had lost the use of their hands.

Her heart ached for the artist who could no longer hold a paint brush, for the carpenter who could no longer swing a hammer, for the mother who could no longer lift her baby. She became an expert at grafting new tendons into the crippled hands. She showed the people how to exercise their hands so that the fingers could do their work again.

Dr. Mary's patients loved her. When they looked into her merry eyes and saw the joy and pain in her face, they received hope again. They knew that Dr. Mary understood. She had been through it herself. She knew how they were suffering, and she was there to help them. Her life of service and Christian faith made them realize that in Christ not only their hands but also their lives could be remade.

## 26.
# Where Shall We Go?
## (P. A. and Elizabeth Penner)
## Around 1900

It was the year 1900. Young Peter A. Penner and his wife Elizabeth had just come all the way from their little Mennonite community in Mountain Lake, Minnesota, to India to be missionaries. How should they start their work? Who would listen to the good news of Christ? They were waiting for God to show them what to do.

One Sunday the P. A. Penners were just about to eat their noon meal of rice and curry, when Elizabeth suddenly said, "Look, Peter, there are two men sitting under our tree."

Peter also looked out the window. Then he and his wife looked at each other. "They have leprosy," said Peter slowly.

They both knew that people sick with leprosy were very unhappy. No one wanted to be near them for fear of also getting the disease. No one wanted to give them a drink or something to eat. They were driven away from home. With their hands and feet all crippled, leprosy patients could not work. They had to beg for food.

It was clear what they had to do. Quickly Elizabeth took some of the rice and curry from the bowl on their table, and Peter carried it out to the hungry men.

Peter and Elizabeth thought the men would leave as people who had leprosy usually did, but at supper time they were still sitting under the tree. They were again holding out their hands for food. Once more Peter and Elizabeth shared their meal.

On Monday morning the sick men were still there.

Peter went out to them. "Why are you staying here?" he asked them. "Why don't you go on as others usually do?"

"Where shall we go?" they asked sadly. "You are kind. We want to stay with you."

Peter knew it was true. They had nowhere to go. No one cared about them.

"Alright," said Peter. "You may stay here and we will see to it that you get shelter and food and some medicine. We shall try to help you."

Word got around very quickly that there were people here who were kind. One day a poor woman came who could hardly walk. A man came who had no fingers. More and more leprosy patients arrived. Peter and Elizabeth soon felt this was how God wanted them to start their work. These were the people God had entrusted to their love and care.

At first they built some huts to shelter the patients and gave them food and clothing. Soon so many people who needed help came that there was not enough room for them. Over the years, with the help of their Mennonite friends in North America, the Mission for Lepers, and the Indian government, P. A. Penner built a big leprosy hospital and home at Champa. At one time there were over five hundred patients there.

At last people sick with leprosy had a place to go. But besides being treated for their disease, they also heard, for the first time the good news that God loved them.

When the P. A. Penners returned to America after forty years of service, there was a large Christian congregation at Champa.

# 27.
# *Your Sins Will Find You Out*
## *(J. F. Kroeker)*
## Around 1900

Chandu was one of the orphan boys enrolled in the Christian boys' school at Janjgir, India. He was glad that he had been accepted there. Finally he had enough to eat and a clean place to sleep, and the missionaries, Mr. and Mrs. J. F. Kroeker, were kind to him. He liked them very much.

Chandu could not quite figure out, however, what all this was that they were being taught in school. For instance, what did the teachers mean by *honesty*? They said the God of heaven and earth did not want you to steal. How odd! Why not take something if you could get away with it? That was only smart, was it not?

One day Chandu happened to be walking past the little storeroom when the missionary Sahib took out a tin of kerosene. Chandu saw there were many more tins of kerosene standing there. Kerosene could easily be sold in the marketplace. Chandu saw an easy way of making some money.

When night came and everyone was asleep, Chandu stole out of the boys' dormitory and ran lightly across the yard to the storeroom. He pried open the locked door and quickly took one of the tins of kerosene. He hid it in the bushes and slipped back to his room. He was sure no one had seen him.

The next morning the voice of Kroeker Sahib suddenly rang out clearly across the missionary compound, "Everyone come here to the verandah at once!"

The boys from the school came. The caretaker of the oxen and cattle came. The water man came. They all came running on their bare feet.

"A tin of kerosene is missing from the storeroom," said the missionary Sahib sadly. "Who has taken it?"

They all shook their heads. Chandu shook his most emphatically. No one was guilty.

"Alright," said the Sahib, his clear eyes looking at each one in turn, "we will find out who took it. There are footprints of bare feet in the dust near the kerosene tins. He whose feet match the footprints is the guilty one."

Chandu became uneasy. His heart was beginning to beat wildly.

First the Sahib called one of the men who had big feet. He had to place his foot near the imprint in the dust. "No, your feet are too big," said the Sahib. "You are not guilty. You may go."

Then the Sahib called one of the little boys. "No, your feet are too small," he said. "They do not match the footprint in the dust. You did not do it."

"Chandu," called the Sahib. "Come and stand beside the footprint."

Chandu came forward. His foot matched the print in the dust exactly.

Chandu looked down. He felt the Sahib's kind hands on his shoulders. Finally Chandu said, "Sahib, I am sorry. I took the tin last night. I will bring it back."

"Good," said Kroeker Sahib. "I am glad you have told me the truth. I forgive you as God has forgiven all of us. But always remember, Chandu, that whatever we do, we leave footprints of some kind behind us. Our sins will find us out. The good we do will also leave an imprint. Always remember that."

Chandu brought back the kerosene. Then the boys went back to school. The men went back to work. The incident was never mentioned again.

# 28.
# *That Others Might Live*
## (Annie Funk)
## Around 1900

Annie Funk was a good teacher. She came to India in 1906, and it didn't take her long to start a school for girls when she found out that there was none for them. Only boys were supposed to be able to learn.

"What nonsense!" thought Annie Funk. "How can we build the church of Jesus Christ in India unless the girls and women can read the Bible?" She set to work and soon had a little group of girls coming to her school. It was a struggle, but the school was coming along well when something unfortunate happened.

Annie Funk received a cable from her pastor in the Hereford Mennonite Church in Bally, Pennsylvania. Her mother was ill and she must come home immediately.

Annie was worried. She packed quickly. Another of the missionaries would teach her school. She said good-bye and started on her long journey home.

In London she changed her ship reservation to go on the S. S. *Titanic* which was scheduled to get her home much sooner. It was March in the year 1912.

The S. S. *Titanic* was a beautiful ship. People said it was so well built that it would never sink. One night, however, it struck a huge iceberg. The ship started filling with water. The people crowded to get into lifeboats, but there were far too few since everybody had believed that the ship would never sink.

Annie Funk finally got near a lifeboat. It was the last one on her deck and it was already filled with people. But there was one place left. Someone helped her in.

Just as the lifeboat was about to be swung

overboard, a woman rushed up to it and cried, "My children! My children!" There was not a single spot left for her.

Annie quickly got up. "Let me out," she said. "That mother must have my seat."

The lifeboat, with the mother on board, soon was on its way to safety, but Annie was left standing on the deck.

Soon after that the S. S. *Titanic* sank.

Annie"s mother, her friends and relatives in Bally, Pennsylvania, were deeply shocked and saddened when they heard the tragic news of Annie's death.

Many churches held services in memory of her. Her own congregation placed a stone marker in the cemetery as a memorial.

People in India felt they wanted to honor Annie in a different way. They did not put a marker in a cemetery but built a large school for girls in memory of their first teacher, Annie Funk.

Soon shouts and laughter of happy India girls rang through the new school, called *Annie Funk Memorial School.* More girls than Annie had ever dreamed would come to her little school, now had a chance to learn to read and write and hear the good news of Jesus Christ. Thousands of girls that over the years graduated from this school became teachers, nurses, mothers, and evangelists who helped to build the church in India.

# 29.
# *Who Will Help US?*
## *(Ezra and Elizabeth Steiner)*
## Around 1914

In the village of Sukhri in India lived a weaver named Gopal and his family. Gopal had not always lived in Sukhri. He and his friend Sunadher had brought their families to Sukhri because they had heard of new lands being opened up in the jungle there.

The two families were glad to live in Sukhri, but they missed being with other Christians. No people in the village had ever heard about Christ. Gopal and Sunadher and their families, who were Christians, were very lonely. They tried to tell others the good news but they did not know enough about it themselves. They needed teachers.

One day Gopal heard of missionaries who lived eighty miles to the west in Raipur. At last! Gopal was sure he could get help there. it was hot, but Gopal set out without delay to walk through the jungle to Raipur.

"Will you send some teachers to Sukhri to teach us about Christ?" he asked when he arrived. "We need you."

The missionary Sahib was kind, but he said, "I am sorry, Gopal, we would very much like to help you, but Sukhri is not in our territory. We cannot come to you."

Sadly Gopal walked the eighty miles home again. He wanted his children to learn the stories about Jesus in the Bible. He wanted his neighbors to hear them. He knew what a difference it made in his life. Could no one help them?

A year later Gopal heard of missionaries 110 miles to the southeast. Gopal was determined. Christ had sought and found him. He must now seek Christ. He walked all the way to Balingir where the missionaries lived.

"Please send some Christian teachers to us in Sukhri," he pleaded .

The missionary Sahib was very kind, but he said, "I am sorry, Gopal, but Sukhri is too far away from here. None of the evangelists will go that far into the jungle. We cannot help you."

Again Gopal had to return home without the good news. He was discouraged, but each day he prayed, "Lord Jesus, send us the servant you will choose."

About a year later, Gopal and his friend Sunadher went to a marketplace in a city to buy thread for their weaving. Suddenly they heard some singing. Why, it was a Christian song!

The two friends hurried toward a little group of missionaries who had set up camp there. "Surely these are people of God," Gopal thought. "They will help us."

After the preaching, they walked over to the Indian evangelist who was with the missionaries. His name was Isa Das. "We are weavers from Sukhri," they said. "Could you not send us some teachers to show us the way of Christ?"

Isa Das immediately took them to the tent where the missionaries Ezra and Elizabeth Steiner were handing out medicine to the sick.

"Please come to our village," the weavers begged. "We need you."

Ezra and Elizabeth looked at each other. This was the last stop on a long preaching tour. They were exhausted. Their supplies were used up. Their baby was getting cranky, and at home on the mission station many duties were waiting for them.

"We are sorry," they said. "We cannot come now. We must be home by Saturday."

This time Gopal would not be turned away. "Then send someone to teach our children," he said. "We are ignorant. We don't want our children to grow up that way."

"But we have no one to send," said Ezra and Elizabeth sadly.

That evening the missionaries conducted their last service. They showed pictures. They preached. Gopal and Sunadher were there again. They came to the missionaries. They lay down on the ground with their faces in the dust and pleaded, "Please come with us. Tell our people about Christ. Is there no hope for us?"

Wearily Ezra and Elizabeth shook their heads. They could not come.

Gopal stayed that night with Isa Das, the Indian evangelist. The next morning Gopal and Sunadher again approached the missionaries. The missionary party was all packed up and ready to start traveling through the jungle on the long way home.

"Please come!" Gopal begged. "Must our children grow up in ignorance, darkness, and fear?" he said. "They need a Savior."

Gopal saw Ezra and Elizabeth looking at each other again. Then Ezra said to this wife, "Elizabeth, I can't stand it anymore. I think God is calling us."

"Yes," said Elizabeth, "I feel the same way, but what shall we do?"

The two missionaries bowed their heads in prayer. Then Elizabeth took the baby, got on the cart without her husband, and the party started out into the jungle on the way home. Ezra Steiner went with Gopal and Sunadher to the faraway village of Sukhri.

Ezra was the first white missionary the people there had ever seen. They were eager to hear him. They were eager to hear the good news of salvation. They felt the presence of Christ among them.

That was the beginning of the Christian church in Sukhri. An outstation was started there. The Indian evangelist Isa Das and his gifted wife Mathuria Bai faithfully ministered to the people. Years later there were thousands of Christians in that area.

## 30.
# Who Killed the Rooster?
## Around 1970

One day a man came to the door of missionaries Jake and Dorothy Giesbrecht in India. The man was distressed. He was crying.

"What is wrong?" asked Jake.

"My rooster has been killed. A wild cat came from the jungle and ate it," said the man, looking down. "I was going to sell the rooster so I could buy some clothing for my son. I want my son to go to school. I want him to learn something. And now the rooster is dead. Tell me, who killed the rooster—God or Satan?"

"What do you think?" asked Jake.

"I don't know. I don't know," said the man sorrowfully. "But I had a dream. And in the dream God told me that my son would be educated even though it would be very difficult."

"Is the answer God gave you good enough for you?" asked Jake.

"Yes," said the man slowly. "Yes, it is."

The man's son went to school and received an education just like the man had been told in his dream.

## 31.
# I Want to Go Back
## (Annelle Wiens)
## 1981

Annelle Wiens and her friend, Enid Janzen, were missionary children. They had both gone to Woodstock, a school high up in the mountains of India, and so now, back in North America and grown up, they often dreamed of going to visit their old school again.

"Enid," said Annelle one day, "guess what! My parents are planning to go back to India for a visit. Let's go with them and then stay on in Woodstock for a while."

"Great!" said Enid immediately. "But what would we do in Woodstock? We can't go to school there anymore."

"Well," thought Annelle, "maybe we could help with something there—do voluntary service work."

That is how the idea of going to India to do volunteer work was born.

In time all the arrangements were made. They could not help in Woodstock School, but after traveling for six weeks with Annelle's parents, they would work for six weeks in the mission school at Korba, and then do voluntary service work for six weeks in Calcutta. The two girls were jubilant.

The first six weeks when they were traveling around with Annelle's parents in India were great. But then, suddenly, they were all alone. Annelle's parents had gone home to North America, and the two girls were on their own. There they stood among the milling crowds of India trying to board a train to Korba. They

**47**

were frightened. But it was also exciting to have to make all decisions by themselves .

In Korba they were suddenly faced by huge classes of children. There were about fifty very lively children in one room. In one room there were seventy! And Annelle and Enid were supposed to teach them English. The two girls had no teacher training. It was overwhelming. They did not know how to discipline the children. How could they stand six weeks of this?

But something in the school made them very happy. They loved the children and the children loved them. "Good morning, Miss! Good morning, Miss!" the children would shout from everywhere, and someone always had a rose for them to put in their hair or on their saris.

Another thing that made their stay in Korba very meaningful was that they could live with Helen and Samuel Stephen, an Indian couple, and so experience the Indian way of life.

For the next six weeks they worked in Calcutta. They saw the terrible poverty. They saw people who were sick, who were starving, who were dying. But they also saw people who were filled with the love of Christ and who helped the poor.

In the mornings Annelle and Enid helped to take care of the little children in Mother Teresa's orphanage. Here were children who had been left on the street or in a hospital by their parents who could not take care of them anymore. Here were little children, who, though they now had a roof over their heads and something to eat, had no one to love them, to talk to them, to help them learn to walk. There were far too few workers in the orphanage for so many children.

Annelle and Enid helped to wash the children and to feed them. Then they held them or played with them. They helped them learn to walk. The children were so starved for love that they clung to the girls and screamed when they put them down.

Annelle and Enid would sit on the floor and hold as many children on their laps as possible. The children fought for the space. They all wanted to be loved.

Annelle especially tried to help a beautiful lit-tle girl called Tara who was retarded. Annelle loved her so much that it was hard for her to leave her, especially when she saw Tara was beginning to respond to her and smile and laugh.

In the afternoons, the girls went to different places where the poor, the helpless, and the sick were cared for. Then they reported to the Mennonite Central Committee how the programs were working and what kind of help was needed.

All too soon the weeks in India were over and it was time for Annelle and Enid to return to America. Their plan to stay at Woodstock School had been impossible. Instead, they had received something much better. They had received a world of experiences that helped them see the need of human beings and the opportunities of helping them.

"It made me grow up," said Annelle. you see such need, then you know you have to help the whole person—both physically and spiritually. I hated the poverty and yet I loved being there. I miss that life. This I know for sure—someday if I can, I will go back to India or to some other place to help."

## 32.
# Whoever Sows Sparingly Will Reap Sparingly

The following story is told in India.

Once there was a Brahman who was both wealthy and very religious. He always wanted to receive rather than to give. He put rice from his house in a bag, and said, "I will take this rice and beg. People will think that the rice was already given to me by others."

On the way he met the king.

"Oh, great king," said the Brahman, "will you give me a gift?"

"No," said the king. "You give me a gift."

Since the Brahman had always received and had never learned to give, he asked himself, "How much shall I give?" He reached into his bag and gave the king one grain of rice.

Both returned to their houses. When the Brahman looked at his rice, he found one grain of gold.

"Where did this come from?" he cried in surprise. "It must be the kernel of rice that I gave to the king!"

He immediately ran out to find the king to give him all his rice, but the king had disappeared.

Sadly the Brahman thought to himself, "I gave a little and this is what I got. If I had given all, how rich I would be now!"

# The Good News
# in China

# 33.
# *An Answer to Prayer*
## *(Hudson Taylor)*
## 1832

First of all, the fact that Hudson Taylor was a boy was an answer to prayer. His father, James Taylor, wanted very much to be a missionary and could not. So he prayed that if he were ever to have a son, that son might go out and bring the good news of Jesus Christ to many who had never heard it. On May 21, 1832, a son was born to James and Amelia Taylor in Yorkshire, England. They named him Hudson.

At first it did not seem possible that little Hudson would ever become a missionary. He was frail and so often sick that he could go to school only two years before he was fourteen. His father taught him at home. He learned the Hebrew alphabet sitting on his father's lap before he was four!

Hudson was a bright happy boy, and very affectionate. In his home everything was orderly and beautifully clean. He learned to be that way from his mother. His father was very honest and thought it was wrong to be in debt. From him, Hudson learned to be truthful and careful in business matters. From both his parents he learned to love the Bible, to pray, and to trust God completely. His mother and father always looked to God for his will and guidance in every decision of life. Hudson knew that.

Hudson's new birth was also an answer to prayer. Both his mother and sister had been in special prayer for his conversion. At seventeen, Hudson experienced the incredible joy and peace of new life with Christ. This helped to give Hudson the faith that God really answers prayer.

This was important, for Hudson Taylor did become a missionary. He went to China and eventually organized the China Inland Mission. He had to depend on God to supply his needs.

When he talked about God he usually called him *Father.*

Hudson Taylor asked his heavenly Father for workers. He asked him for funds. He asked him for strength to overcome the tremendous difficulties connected with the work in China.

God heard him. The China Inland Mission grew so much that finally more missionaries went to China under that organization than under any other agency, Roman Catholic or Protestant. Tens of thousands in China heard the good news because Hudson Taylor inspired so many people to go out and tell others about Christ.

# 34.
# *Bring Them In*
## (Gladys Aylward)
## Around 1925

Yangcheng was a very old city. To Gladys Aylward, a young missionary who had just arrived from England, it seemed unbelievably beautiful. There it was, almost like a nest built on the saddle between two mountains. Gladys and her guide, both on mules, were struggling up the steep trail that led to its ancient gate. With her heart beating wildly, Gladys looked up at the Chinese city where she would tell the people about Christ. Finally her great dream was to be fulfilled.

Gladys was a very new missionary. She did not yet know how difficult it is to tell the good news about Jesus when no one cares to hear it.

She lived with a very old missionary, Mrs. Lawson, in a broken-down old building. Every time they came out of their building, the little children on the street fled in all directions. They were afraid. The older children jeered in a sing-song voice. Grown-ups threw mud and dirt at them. Everybody called them *lao-yang-kwei* or "foreign devils." How could they ever win their confidence? How could they ever get them to listen to the good news they had brought?

One day Gladys and Mrs. Lawson were walking through the narrow main street of the city. The mule trains were already coming through the gates to find food and lodging at one of the inns within the city wall. Yangcheng was on an important trade route and so for hundreds of years it had been the stopping place for the muleteers and their caravans.

As the two missionaries stepped aside to let the mules go by, Gladys said, "I wish we could talk to these men. They would carry our message far and wide on their trade route."

Mrs. Lawson looked at Gladys in surprise.

Then after a bit she said, "Why, that's it. We will open an inn."

"What?" Gladys could not believe her ears.

"Of course," continued Mrs. Lawson. "Our old house was used as a stopping place for muleteers and their animals hundreds of years ago. All we need to do is fix up the building and use it that way again."

At first Gladys could not understand how running an inn had anything to do with proclaiming the good news, but Mrs. Lawson said, "But don't you see? Once we have the men and their animals inside the courtyard, we can tell them the stories about Jesus. The Chinese love stories. We will give them a bed and food for the same price as in other places, but as an extra, we will tell them stories."

Gladys and Mrs. Lawson went to work. The rubble in the courtyard was cleaned out. The roof was mended. The doors were fixed. Over the gate they hung a new yellow signboard painted with Chinese characters in black and gold. It said *The Inn of Eight Happinesses.*

Yang, their kind Chinese helper, prepared a big kettle of delicious food. You could smell it all the way down the street. They were open for business.

Gladys and Mrs. Lawson waited anxiously for the first customers. Finally they saw the first mule train of the day coming down the street. Would it turn in at their place? No, it crowded into the inn on the opposite side of the street. The men did not even look at the sign. They gave no indication that they smelled their good food.

One after another the caravans came into the city. All went plodding past. Not even one looked at the Inn of Eight Happinesses. They were obviously all boycotting the house of the "foreign devils."

Gladys and Mrs. Lawson sat down sadly. They discussed what they should do.

Finally Mrs. Lawson had an idea. She pointed her finger straight at tiny five-foot Gladys and said, "You are the one. You will have to drag them in!"

"Drag them in? I drag them in?" Gladys was horrified, but Mrs. Lawson was already chattering away with Yang in Chinese. Yang nodded. He was wise. He knew the way of his countrymen, and he agreed.

When the lead mule passed by, Gladys was to grab for its head and drag it in the direction of their courtyard. All the other animals, which were tied to the head mule, would then follow. And once the mules were headed in the direction of food no one could stop them, not even their drivers.

"But if the mules bite me?" protested Gladys.

"Don't be silly," said Mrs. Lawson. "They won't. I am too old to do it. Yang will be busy with the food. You are the only one."

The next night, Gladys stood in the door way of the inn waiting for business. Yang had taught her a few Chinese words to call out as invitation: "We have no bugs. We have no fleas. Good, good, good. Come, come, come!"

But no one paid any attention to little Gladys standing there. After three caravans had passed by, she made the awful decision. Another mule train came plodding along. She made a desperate leap for the lead mule's head. At that instant, the muleteer saw the "foreign devil" near him. He screamed in terror, but he couldn't escape because he had the rein tied to his wrist. Gladys jerked the mule's head into her courtyard and, sure enough, all the rest of the animals followed, as well as the one man who couldn't get away. All the other muleteers had fled.

Mrs. Lawson and Yang came out of the house, delighted. "Well done," said Mrs. Lawson running up to her, "Well done!" But when the one muleteer saw Mrs. Lawson's white hair, he shrieked. That was too much for him. He tore the rein from his wrist and also fled.

Yang went into the city to find the muleteers. He explained to them that these white ladies were not dangerous. "See," he said, "I, an old and respected Chinese, live at their house and I am unharmed. They offer you good beds, good food, and even stories free of charge."

Yang knew that no human being could make those mules leave the courtyard until next morning, and he knew that the muleteers knew that also. And they would not leave their mules. They were too valuable.

Slowly the muleteers came back. They took the packs down. They fed and watered the animals. They came into the large room. Yang brought in the steaming food. They ate it. "Good!" they muttered.

When Gladys and Mrs. Lawson came in, they all tried to move away to the back of the rooms, but Mrs. Lawson said cheerfully, "Don't be afraid. I want to tell you a story and all stories here are free."

The muleteers began to look interested.

Mrs. Lawson sat down on a stool.

"A long, long time ago," she began, "there lived in the country of Palestine a man called Jesus Christ. . ."

The men listened spellbound. Storytelling had begun at the Inn of Eight Happinesses. No men had to be dragged in after that.

## 35.
# On the Way to the Promised Land
## (Gladys Aylward)
## Around 1939

Over the years, the Chinese people had come to love and respect Gladys Aylward, the small missionary from England. At first they were frightened when they saw her and called her "foreign devil," but now they had given her the name *Ai-weh-deh*, which meant "the Virtuous One." They started calling her *Ai-weh-deh* when they realized that she loved children and that she helped them whenever she could.

Gradually more and more hungry, homeless children gathered around Gladys. Ai-weh-deh always had room for one more. Finally she had a hundred children in the old mission house.

Gladys had many happy days with the children. But now she was worried. War had broken out in China. The Japanese were coming closer and closer. The children were in grave danger. What could she do to save them? She had to make a decision.

There were high mountains all around them. Safety lay on the other side of the Yellow or Hwang Ho River many miles away. How could she take a hundred children, some of them four and five years old, over those rugged peaks? It was madness. And yet it seemed the only way.

She called the children together.

"Tomorrow morning we are all starting on a long, long walk to get away from the war," she told them. "Everybody must go to bed early. When you get up tomorrow tie your bedding in a roll and take your bowl and chopsticks with you."

The children chattered happily. To go for a long walk with Ai-weh-deh would be fun. They scampered off to bed.

The next morning they were all up when the sun rose, wild with excitement and ready to go. Gladys had a little whistle with which she could call the children together. She lined them all up and had a roll call to see that no one was missing.

Then they set out down the trail leading south. For a while they could follow the trail, but then they would have to head into the wild mountains.

"How many days will it take us to reach the Yellow River?" asked one of the fifteen-year-old girls a little anxiously.

"The muleteers traveling on the regular trail take five days," said Gladys. "Since we have to walk right through the mountains, it will probably take us twelve days.

At first things went quite well. The children even climbed up and down rocks and ran to explore side paths. At noon they ate some of the millet that they had brought along. But as the afternoon wore on, more and more often a little one would steal close to Gladys, hang on to her coat and say, "Ai-weh-deh, I am tired." "Ai-weh-deh, my feet hurt." "Ai-weh-deh, let's go home now."

Gladys and the older boys took turns carrying the little ones. At last they came to a village. Fortunately an old Buddhist priest saw them straggling by his temple and invited them to stay for the night.

The next morning everyone was rested and they could start on their way again. But things got rougher and rougher. The mountains were so rugged that sometimes the older children had to hand the little ones one by one in a relay up or down big cliffs. Shoes wore out and so feet got very sore. They ran out of food. They were thirsty most of the time for it was hot and water was hard to find. At night they huddled in the shelter of some big rock. But in the morning they went on again.

Whenever they reached a level stretch of ground, Gladys would start to sing a hymn and they would all bravely march along, singing the chorus. Oh, surely, surely they would soon reach the Yellow River beyond which lay freedom!

On the twelfth day they saw it! Far away the river glistened in the sunshine. And close by they saw a village. At last they would get some food. Singing, the ragged little band of children marched toward it.

But what was this? It seemed very odd. There were no people. The village was deserted. Probably all the people had left because of the war.

Gladys would not give up. She blew her whistle and lined up the children. The littlest one she took on her back, and off they trudged. "We shall go to the river and catch a boat," she said. "We shall be safe on the other side."

But when they reached the river no boat was in sight. They hoped one would come from the other side to get them. They waited and waited. The older boys went back to the deserted village to look for leftover food.

Day after day, night after night under the stars, they waited. "Ai-weh-deh, we're hungry," the children whimpered. "Ai-weh-deh, when are we going to cross the river?"

Gladys tried to comfort them. She told them stories. They sang together. But all the time, they watched the river. When would a boat come?

On the fourth day there was a mood of despair over the whole group.

But suddenly one of the children crept up to Gladys and said, "Ai-weh-deh, remember how Moses took the children of Israel through the Red Sea? Why does God not open the Yellow River for us to cross?"

Gladys pressed the little girl to her. Then she said, "You and I will kneel down and ask him."

They did. Then Gladys started all the children singing again. Suddenly some of the children jumped up. "A soldier, a soldier, Ai-weh-deh!" they shouted. There coming toward them was a Chinese officer who was patrolling the area and who had heard the unbelievable sound of children singing.

"Are you mad?" he asked Gladys. "Who are you and what are you doing with all these children here on the enemy side of the river?"

"We are refugees and we are trying to cross the river," said Gladys.

The officer immediately called for boats. When they came, Gladys and the children piled in.

It was not long before they were safe on the other side.

36.

# Nest-in-the-Clouds

Nest-in-the-Clouds is the real name of a village high in the mountains of China. Many of the people in the village live in caves or in houses built right into the hillside.

In one of these houses lived a little girl called Pine Needle. Her parents were the only Christians in the village. All the other people prayed to wooden or iron or paper gods.

When New Year came around, the people of the village came to Pine Needle's home. They said to her father and mother, "You must come to the temple with us to offer incense to the gods.

"No," said Pine Needle's father. "We cannot do that anymore. We are Christians now and pray only to the true God."

"If you don't come with us, something terrible is going to happen to you," said one of the men angrily.

One day not long after that, Pine Needle was watching her mother stir the soup for dinner. The stove was made of bricks and a big round kettle was built into it. Pine Needle was sitting on the edge of the stove. She bent over to smell the soup. Suddenly she slipped and fell. One arm was scalded in the boiling soup.

There was no medicine in the house and no doctor in the whole area. Pine Needle cried all day and into the night because the pain was so bad. Soon she had a high fever. Nobody knew what to do.

The neighbors of course said, "See, didn't we tell you? It happened because you did not give your offering to the gods!"

Pine Needle's parents knew that was not the reason for the accident, but how could they help their neighbors understand this? And how could they help their little girl?

"We must bring Pine Needle to the mission station," said her father.

Quickly they wrapped her in warm blankets. Her father took her in his arms and after praying together and saying good-bye to Mother, they rode away on their donkey.

Finally, toward evening, they arrived at the mission station. The doctor was not at home. The missionary said, "There is a hospital a hundred miles from here. You must take Pine Needle there on the train, or she will die. I will help you pay for the trip."

So Father took Pine Needle to the strange white house in the city called a hospital. He had never seen anything like it.

The doctor said to him, "We need to graft some skin on your daughter's arm. Would you be willing to give your skin for this purpose?"

Pine Needle's father thought giving your skin meant giving your life. What a terrible decision to make! He prayed to God to give him strength. Finally he came back to the doctor and said,

"Yes, I am willing. The Lord Jesus gave his life for me. I will give my skin for my child."

After a long while, Pine Needle's father awoke in his clean white hospital bed. "Am I in heaven?" he asked the nurse.

"In heaven!" she exclaimed. "Why, no! Did you think you would die?"

"Yes," he said. "Did I not give my skin for my daughter?"

"Yes, but only a little piece of it," the nurse explained. "You will soon be well—much sooner than your child."

Pine Needle's father praised God for his help. He decided he would tell his neighbors about how wonderfully his heavenly Father had given him and his daughter life again.

Three months later, Pine Needle and her father returned home to the little village, Nest-in-the-Clouds, high in the mountains.

The neighbors had long since given up ever seeing them again. Pine Needle's mother had never stopped praying, however, and welcomed them with indescribable joy. The neighbors crowded around in astonishment.

"See my arm," said Pine Needle.

"And see my leg," said her father. He told them the whole story. "I gave my skin for my child."

The neighbors were deeply touched. Such love for a daughter in a country where a girl was worth very little was completely new to them.

"Tell us about your God!" they said.

The time had come. At last Pine Needle's father could tell them the good news that Jesus Christ loved them so much that he gave his life on the cross for them.

Now they could not hear enough. They invited the missionaries to come and tell them more. Soon almost all the people in the village had thrown away their gods and decided to worship the true God. They wanted to belong to a God who answers prayers.

# 37.
# *A Great Secret*
## (H. J. Brown)
## Around 1900

Henry Brown had a secret. A big secret. Henry did not even tell his father, though he did not know exactly why. He only knew that it was so sacred that he did not dare tell any human being. It belonged to his Lord and him.

Henry was only eleven years old when the very strong conviction came over him that he should become a missionary to tell the good news of Jesus to people in other lands. This call of God came so naturally and yet so strongly that he never doubted it nor resisted it. It filled his heart with joy and longing. Henry J. Brown knew what he was going to do with his life.

First of all, he knew that he must have a good preparation for such important work. He must get a good education. But that was very difficult. His family was poor. From the time that Henry was ten he had to work during the summer for other people to help support his family. He could not save money for high school and college.

It was seldom that a missionary came to his home town in Mountain Lake, Minnesota. But one Sunday when Henry was about seventeen years old, the minister in his church preached on missions. "Is there no one in this big audience who will volunteer to be the Lord's messenger?" the minister called. "Is there not a single one who will say, 'Here am I, send me'?"

Henry almost jumped to his feet. In his heart he was saying, "Yes, yes, Lord. I will go!" He was too shy to say it in public, but the challenging words of the minister encouraged him to keep on working toward his goal.

Henry had to work hard for his education.

He lengthened his summer vacations in order to earn more money, and so when he finally got to school in fall the class was far ahead of him. He needed to make up the work which he had missed and so he had to work much harder than the others. Besides going to high school he worked in boardinghouses and restaurants to earn extra money. If he was to do his homework, he had to do it at night.

But Henry Brown had a goal he must reach. Words that helped him in those days were the ones from "The Ladder of St. Augustine" by Longfellow. "Heights by great men reached and kept/Were not attained by sudden flight,/but they, while their companions slept,/Were toiling upward in the night."

Henry struggled on to prepare himself for the mission field. He went to college and seminary. Sometimes things were so difficult that he wondered whether he would ever get to a foreign country.

One evening, while he was praying, Henry Brown received a vision. His dark room was suddenly light. High before him in the air he saw a big cross and above it a beautiful golden crown. Under the crown he saw the words, "Your reward," and under the cross, "You must work hard."

Hard work and a big cross was what God assigned to H. J. Brown and his wife Maria. They started the General Conference Mennonite mission in China. They worked there for forty years and saw their feeble beginnings grow into a flourishing mission with churches, schools, and hospitals. Many other missionaries came to join them.

But, finally all missionaries had to leave

China because of the civil war. That seemed the biggest cross of all. But the H. J. Browns knew that over the cross there was a crown.

The crown they cherished most was the memory of all those dear Chinese friends who had heard and accepted the good news of salvation.

# 38.
# *All Idols Have to Go*
## *(H. J. and Maria Brown)*
## Around 1930

A long time ago in China, missionaries H. J. and Maria Brown were meeting in a distant town. At the close of the meeting a man by the name of a Mr. Liu came to them.

"Please come and visit my home before you go back," he said.

The missionaries were eager to get started on their homeward journey, but Mr. Liu insisted. Somehow the Browns felt that Mr. Liu had a special reason for this invitation, but they did not ask. They went with him to his house.

When they arrived in the front yard, Mr. Liu first ushered them into a room and they were served tea. Then Mr. Liu took Mrs. Brown into the backyard to meet his wife. When he came back he insisted the Mr. Brown come too.

Mr. Brown thought they should be starting for home, but Mr. Liu would not listen to any excuses.

On their way to the backyard they first came to the kitchen. Mr. Liu pointed to the kettle god pasted on the wall right above the kettle. "It is enough!" he said. "Tear him down. He has made me suffer enough. For years I have been tormented by the evil ones. Now I believe in Jesus. He has set me free and healed me. All idols have to go, for I will worship only the Savior. These powers of darkness have to go."

Mr. Brown took down the kitchen or kettle god.

While he was doing that, Mr. Liu ran into the next room and fetched the god of riches.

Both the kitchen god and the god of riches were thrust into the stove.

After both gods had burned to ashes, Mr. Liu said, "Now that they are gone, let the missionary lead us in a word of prayer to the true God."

Mr. Brown prayed with all his heart. Then he and Mrs. Brown went home rejoicing.

# 39.
# *Respect for the Dead*
## Around 1930

Mr. Wong was deeply distressed. His mother had died some time ago, and because he was a Christian, he had given his mother a Christian burial. Now his Chinese non-Christian neighbors were taunting him, "You Christians! You don't love or honor your parents. There was no weeping and wailing at your mother's funeral. You just threw her into a hole in the ground. And now you don't burn any incense in her honor!"

All this hurt Mr. Wong deeply. He had loved his mother with all his heart, but he did not sorrow as if he had no hope. He knew his mother was alive with Jesus Christ. He wanted to worship God and not his ancestors. What should he do to make his neighbors understand about the Christian faith?

Mr. Wong thought deeply about this for a long time. There must be a Christian way of showing the love and respect he had for the memory of his dear mother.

Finally he got a good idea. He was a pharmacist. Often he saw poor people coming into his drugstore. Many did not have enough money to pay for medicine they desperately needed and as a follower of Christ he was concerned about them.

When the first anniversary of his mothers death came around, he made a sacrifice—not a sacrifice of incense to the dead, but a sacrifice of love to the living. To everyone who came into his drugstore for medicine on that day, he gave the medicine free.

"This is in memory of my dear mother," he would say. I rejoice that she is with the Lord, who will someday raise her from the dead."

The people who received the gift of free medicine looked at Mr. Wong in amazement. This was, indeed, a new way of showing respect to those who had died!

## 40.
# *Do You Remember?*
## (Marie J. Regier)
## 1943

Much trouble had come to China. The Japanese had invaded the country. Now there was war and much destruction everywhere.

Little Sam Wang could not go to school anymore. The mission school was closed and the missionaries who had taught there were either gone or were under house arrest. Sam was very sad. He liked going to school.

One day his parents said, "Sam, we have heard that the missionary teacher, Marie Regier, is teaching children in her own home. The Japanese will not let her leave her house but they will allow children to go to her. Would you like to go too?"

Would he ever! From that day on Sam went to the missionary's house to learn. He loved his teacher. He liked the stories she told. He felt good in the house where there was so much love and goodness.

But one day when he came to the missionary's gate, he stopped in his tracks. The Japanese soldiers were taking his beloved teacher, Miss Regier, and Miss Goertz, the nurse, away. Someone whispered, "They are going to a concentration camp."

Miss Regier looked up as she came out of the gate. She smiled. "Good-bye, Sam," she called.

Sam was so shocked he could not say anything. He waved a little bit, and then he quickly turned away because he knew he was going to cry.

His teacher was gone! What were the soldiers going to do to her? He raced home to tell his parents. Everybody was very sad, but no one could do anything about it.

The years went by. Many changes took place in China. Little Sam Wang grew up. He went to medical school and became a doctor. He married and had two little boys of his own. But he never forgot his former teacher. He still wondered what had happened to her and whether she was still alive.

One day, about forty years later, Sam happened to meet a man who had also known the missionaries. The man beamed at Sam and said, "I have good news! We can again write to America and get letters from there. I received a letter from Marie Regier. Do you still remember your teacher?"

Sam could hardly believe his ears. He quickly wrote down the address. When he got home he sat down immediately and wrote, "Dear Teacher, I just received your address and am writing right away. Do you still remember a little boy called Samuel Wang whom you taught when you were under house arrest?" In his letter Sam told his former teacher what happened in his life. He asked her to write to him.

Not very long afterwards Sam received a letter from his former teacher. Yes, she still remembered him. She had not forgotten the past and the good times they had had together so long ago. Once again the doors between Chinese and American Christians were being opened.

# 41.
# *All Power Is Given to Me*
## 1930-1982

Far away in the country of China lived two little girls. One was Chinese and her name was I Wha or Love Flower. Her parents died and so she was adopted by a missionary lady who gave her the name Lucy Jamison. The other little girl's name was Winifred. She was the child of American missionaries in China.

Lucy and Winifred were best friends. From the time they started walking, they played together. They dug tunnels in the sandbox, waded in the brook, and picked bouquets of flowers. They went to school together, and could speak both Chinese and English.

Finally, Winifred returned to America to go to college. Later Lucy came to America also to go to college but after graduation she went back to China. Only once did Winifred see her again. Lucy came all the way to America to be with Winifred on her wedding day.

Then the war came. Lucy and Winifred could not visit each other anymore. The Communist government did not allow any travel back and forth. They did not allow American missionaries in China. They did not even allow letters to be written. They closed all the churches.

In America Winifred often wondered what was happening to Lucy. She missed her very much. She prayed for her.

Thirty years went by. Never once in all those years did Winifred hear from Lucy. But the time came when Americans were again allowed to visit China. Winifred and her husband, Erland Waltner, were planning to go to China on a trip. How Winifred wished she could visit Lucy! But that seemed completely impossible. She had no address. She did not even know whether Lucy was still alive.

Before the Waltners left for China, Winifred's brother-in-law went to Switzerland on church business. While he was there he met a Chinese man, also there on church business. They talked together in English.

"You speak very good English," said Winifred's brother-in-law to the Chinese man.

"Where did you learn it?"

"I learned it from a Chinese woman who had an American name-Lucy Jamison.

"Lucy Jamison!" exclaimed the other. "You mean you know Lucy Jamison?"

"Yes. But how do you know her?"

"I've never met her, but my wife's sister knew her very well," said Winifred's brother-in-law.

To their great astonishment these two men discovered that out of about a billion people in China they both knew Lucy Jamison!

That is how Winifred heard about her friend Lucy again. She got her address, and they wrote to each other. When Winifred and Erland visited China, they went to see Lucy.

Lucy was not a little girl anymore. Her beautiful black hair had become grey. She had been in prison for twenty years because she was a Christian. But her brown eyes were just as full of kindness and joy as they had ever been. Jesus had been with her.

Lucy and Winifred had much to share. Winifred had had four little girls of her own. Lucy had not married but had adopted three little girls just as she had been adopted. After being released from prison, Lucy was now living with the youngest of them and teaching at a university.

When they said good-bye to each other, Winifred said to Lucy, "If I don't see you again on earth, I'll see you in heaven."

Lucy smiled happily and said, "Yes, and it may be sooner than we think."

# 42.
# *The Call Of God*
## (Stephen Lee)
## Around 1940 - 1982

As a little boy Stephen Lee lived in southern China. His mother and father were Christians. His grandmother and grandfather had already been Christians, and so had his great-grandmother and great-grandfather. A hundred years ago American Baptist missionaries had come to that part of China to tell the people about Christ and ever since then the Lee family had been followers of Jesus.

When Stephen was twelve years old he accepted Christ as his personal Savior. He also developed a great longing and desire to become a pastor when he grew up so that he could help people to know Jesus. It was his call from God. In his heart he knew that and he never forgot it.

While Stephen was growing up, a Communist government came into power in China. Government officials closed the churches and Bible schools. They did not like the Christian religion.

Stephen did not know what to do. The call to become a pastor was still there, but how could he get an education? And if he did get an education, where could he be a pastor when there were no churches?

When Stephen was twenty years old he decided to flee from China and go to the free Island of Hong Kong, which belonged to Great Britain, in order to go to Bible school there. His father had already fled to Hong Kong and could perhaps help him.

Since it was dangerous for anyone to know his plans, Stephen told no one, not even his mother and brothers and sisters. One day Stephen just disappeared. He made his way to the harbor from where he could see Hong Kong five miles away across the water.

But some guards saw Stephen. He had no permission to be in the area where he was standing. Quickly they grabbed him and put him into prison. Now what?

Stephen was determined to get out. He looked for any possibility of escape. And one day when they were taking the prisoners to another place, he bolted and ran!

The guards saw him and caught him. Again Stephen was put in prison.

But Stephen would not give up. He had a call from God. He must get out. Again he ran. And this time no one caught him. Stephen made it back to his home.

Two years later Stephen tried again to escape from China. He planned very carefully. With the help of a friend, he got to the harbor without anybody seeing him. Late one night he stood all alone at the edge of the water. It was smooth and dark and mysterious. Five miles in the distance he could see the lights of Hong Kong. Stephen Lee had decided to swim across the channel.

Would he make it? Stephen had learned to swim almost as soon as he had learned to walk. Now he had practiced swimming for years. It seemed that all his life he had prepared for this moment. He was strong. He was confident of his own strength. He knew he could do it.

He plunged in. With long, powerful strokes he started swimming toward Hong Kong. He knew it would take many hours. He swam and swam. But after a long time, he knew he was making no headway. He was swimming in circles. Somehow a current in the water always swung him around so that he could not keep a straight direction.

When Stephen realized this, he became frightened. Even though he was an excellent swimmer he knew now that he could not make it in his own strength. He cried to God,

"Lord, you know I want to go to Hong Kong to go to Bible school. I want to serve you. Help me, Lord, help me!"

That same minute a powerful current in the water caught him and shot him in the right direction. Almost at once, it seemed to him, he reached the Hong Kong shore and fell, completely exhausted, on the beach.

To his horror, however, he did not fall on a sandy beach. He fell on a beach covered with broken oyster shells!

Stephen had escaped the watchful eyes of the men guarding the harbor, he had made it all the way across the channel, but now the oyster shells got him. They cut his body all over. For a while he could not walk, but finally, bruised and bleeding, he staggered to a farmhouse nearby.

When the people there opened the door they banged it shut again. They wanted no refugees at their house.

Stephen painfully limped to the next house. There the people took him in. They gave him food. They gave him water so he could wash. They gave him clothes. When he finally recovered a little, he contacted his father.

At first his father was very happy to see him. But when he found out that Stephen wanted to become a pastor, he was angry. He expected Stephen, as his oldest son, to help him with his business and take responsibility for the family.

"No, Father," said Stephen. "I have already promised God to become a pastor and serve him. I cannot break that promise."

Now Stephen was on his own again. His father would not support him. Penniless, but in faith, Stephen went to the Bible school in Hong Kong. God in his great wisdom had already made provisions.

A year before Stephen landed in Hong Kong, a Mennonite couple, Henry and Marie Becker from Turpin, Oklahoma, had been in Hong Kong on a tour. When they left, they deposited a sum of money with the Mennonite Central Committee office there and said, "This is for some young person who wants to go to Bible school to prepare for the Christian ministry."

So the money was already there, and Stephen Lee received it.

At last he was on the way to becoming a pastor. For four years in Hong Kong and one year in Canada, the Beckers in Oklahoma supported him. Then Stephen returned to Hong Kong to be a pastor in a Chinese church. When he was married, the Beckers came all the way to Hong Kong to attend his wedding.

But that is not all. Stephen Lee became a very special kind of a pastor. He and his wife Sally and their children eventually came to Canada. They started many Chinese churches there. And when the refugees from Vietnam needed a new home, Stephen and Sally were already in Canada to welcome them. Today there is a Chinese Mennonite church in Vancouver, British Columbia, where the Chinese people can find a spiritual home.

Stephen Lee has the vision to start many more Chinese churches in North America. He believes he has been called by God to do that.

# The Good News
# in Southeast Asia

# 43.

# I Forgive You

## (Ann and Adoniram Judson)
## Around 1820

To be a missionary in a foreign culture is always hard, but Ann and Adoniram Judson, in Burma in the early 1800s, surely had more than their share of difficulties.

The officials, who were against Christianity, were very cruel. People were afraid to be seen with the Judsons. They knew they would be persecuted if they became Christians. Only a few came secretly to ask about the Savior the Judsons were so eager to introduce to them.

During the first five years there was not a single convert. How could the church of Jesus Christ ever be built in Burma?

Ann and Adoniram kept on working faithfully as best they could. Finally Ann had a class of about twenty women who wanted to know more about this God who loved women as much as men. They were utterly astounded at this news.

In spite of the danger, several men and women eventually became followers of Jesus. Adoniram worked hard at translating the New Testament into the Burmese language so the people could read the good news of Jesus for themselves.

Then war broke out between Britain and Burma. The Burmese were immediately suspicious of the English-speaking missionaries. What were they doing in their country? Perhaps they were spies?

One day in June 1824, when Ann and Adoniram were eating their dinner, the door was rudely opened and an official marched in to arrest Adoniram. He tied Adoniram so tightly with a small hard cord, used by the Burmese as an instrument of torture, that he could hardly breathe. Then he was dragged off to prison and flung into a dark filthy room crowded with condemned criminals.

Ann was closely guarded at home so that she could not leave the house. She was almost beside herself with anxiety about her husband. What was happening to him?

Finally Ann was able to get permission from the governor to visit her husband. She hurried to the prison. When she came to the door, Ann saw her husband crawling toward her over the filthy floor, the heavy chains with which he was bound, clanking with every move. His face, unwashed and unshaven, was haggard, but bright with unbelievable joy when he saw her. He had been tortured with fears of what was happening to her, alone and unprotected.

On the next visit to the prison Ann carried a pillow, so hard and uncomfortable that even the jailer did not want it. Into it she had sewn Adoniram's manuscript of the New Testament. It was the only copy, and it was not safe at their house. If it were found, many years, work would be lost.

Adoniram was in that prison for eighteen months. All that time Ann took care of the little group of Christians and tried to get food and clothing to her husband who would otherwise have starved. But, most of all, she tried to get Adoniram out of prison.

She went to the homes of members of the royal family. She knocked at the doors of government officials. She even dared to go to the governor himself. Disregarding any danger to herself, she pleaded everywhere for Adoniram's release.

One of the officials kept her waiting from early morning till noon to see him, and then dismissed her petition with contempt. More than that, as he turned to go, he ordered her to give him her silk umbrella. It was terribly hot in Burma during the noon hour. It was dangerous to walk unprotected from the sun. Ann gave the man her umbrella, but asked if he could not give her a paper umbrella in exchange. He laughed cruelly and would not even do that.

One day when Ann went to see her husband, the prison was empty. All the prisoners had been taken away. The pillow which contained the precious manuscript was also gone.

Ann hurried to the governor. "You can do nothing more for your husband," he said. "Just take care of yourself."

But Ann would not give up. She went through the city streets until she found someone who had seen the prisoners being marched away. Then, taking the Burmese children who were in her care and her own baby, she walked in the same direction. Finally she found the prison where Adoniram had been taken.

More trouble was on the way.

The children got smallpox. Adoniram had a terrible fever. Ann, with the help of a loyal Burmese friend, nursed them back to health. Finally she herself became very ill. She would have died if the Burmese friend had not taken care of her.

After some time Britain won the war.

Adoniram was released from prison. And when the British and the Burmese held a cere-monial dinner to mark the acceptance by the Burmese of the British peace terms, both Ann and Adoniram were invited.

The Burmese officials who had jeered and tormented Ann when she asked them for help were there. The man who had so cruelly taken her umbrella was there. When they saw Ann, they turned pale. Now she could take revenge on them. That is what they would have done in her place.

But Ann looked compassionately at the frightened officials. In pure musical Burmese she said to them, "You have nothing to fear from me. I forgive you." For the first time in their lives they saw what it means to be a Christian.

And what about the precious manuscript? Was it really lost? No! The jailer had torn off the first covering, but had thrown away what to him was a useless hard roll. One of the Burmese Christians recognized the roll as belonging to the Judsons, and had taken it away with him. The translation of the New Testament was safe.

That was the beginning of the Christian church in Burma. A hundred years after Ann and Adoniram struggled so hard to lay the foundation, the Protestant church in Burma had 117,000 members.

## 44.
# *Why Did He Do It?*
## *(Luke and Dorothy Beidler)*
## Around 1976

The Mennonite church in Indonesia needed someone to help work with people who had never heard about Christ. So the church asked the Mennonite Central Committee (MCC) to send them a couple from North America to work together with an Indonesian couple in an outlying village.

Luke and Dorothy Beidler heard the call and went to Indonesia. Soon they became very good friends with the Christian Indonesian couple with whom they worked. They did everything together.

One day the Indonesian man suddenly became very sick. He needed to be taken to a hospital at once. But in Indonesia someone always has to go along to the hospital to take care of the patient—to cook his meals, to wash him, to carry out the bedpan, and to attend to all his needs. The hospital does not do that.

The big question now was who should go along with the sick man. His wife could not go because they had a baby to care for. Both the man's parents and the woman's parents lived very far away on a different island. There wasn't even time to send them a message. As Luke and Dorothy talked it over with the other couple, it became clear to all that Luke was the person who should accompany his co-worker.

The other people there were surprised when the white man stayed by the bedside of the Indonesian. They were amazed when the white man cooked the patient's supper. They couldn't believe their eyes when they saw the white man carry out the bedpan.

They started whispering. They had never seen anything like this happening before. A white man stoop this low and serve an Indonesian? Never! What could this mean?

Now they were all wondering what would happen at night. Since the hospitals are always so crowded, the relative or friend taking care of the sick person always sleeps under the patient's bed. Would this strange white man do this also?

Yes, he did! Luke calmly crawled under the bed of his co-worker and lay down to sleep, just like the Indonesian helpers did.

Word of this event spread throughout the whole island like wildfire. People started asking questions. Who were these white people who would do such a thing? And why were they doing it?

When the sick man was well and both he and Luke were at home again, the two couples, one white and one Indonesian, working together, received calls from surrounding villages saying, "Come and tell us about Jesus."

# 45.
# *The Church That Grew and Grew*
## *(Abdi Djajadihardja)*
## Around 1970

The people in the Semarang Church in Indonesia were glad that they could get together to worship God and to share each other's joys and sorrows. But every once in a while a student would come from the Satya Wacana Christian University some distance away to worship with them and before leaving would say, "Oh, this was good. If only we had a church like this in Salatiga!"

The people in Semarang began wondering whether they should not be doing something so that the students could have a church of their own.

Finally they decided to send a young pastor, Abdi Djajadihardja, to the university town to meet with the students there.

Young Abdi was excited about going, but also a little afraid. Would any of the students come? Would they really want a church? Would he know the right words to say? He prayed to God that the Spirit might guide them every step of the way.

A little group of students gathered around Pastor Abdi Djajadihardja. Soon they were laughing and talking. They called the pastor *Pak Abdi. You* could tell they liked him. Together they read the Bible and prayed and sang.

The next Sunday when Pak Abdi came, there were many more students. Not only that, there were several families who had come to worship.

Every Sunday more and more people came. One Sunday Pak Abdi saw, to his surprise, a Javanese family and a Chinese family in the service. Usually the Javanese and the Chinese people on the island did not like each other too well. Pak Abdi was thrilled. The love of Christ was uniting them all.

The little church in Salatiga grew so fast that soon Pak Abdi moved there permanently to be their full-time pastor. They had always met in someone's home but now the group became much too large. The people built a building.

After a few years that building was too small.

The congregation built a larger shell over the small church. That way they could meet in the old church while they were building the new one. When the large church was almost completed, they tore down the little church and carried it out.

The Salatiga Church knew that the Spirit of God was working mightily among them. They wanted to carry the good news about Jesus Christ to others as well. Pak Abdi and others from the congregation started twelve preaching and teaching missions in outlying villages.

It was just as if the little plant that had been planted in Salatiga by the Semarang Church had now produced twelve new shoots. All those shoots were growing well and would probably soon have new shoots too.

Pak Abdi and the Semarang congregation which had first sent young Pastor Abdi to Salatiga were amazed. They thanked God for the miracle of growth.

# 46.
# *The Bible on the Table*
## (Rosella Toews)
## Around 1975

Rosella Toews, a nurse, was working with the Mennonite Central Committee (MCC) in Bangladesh. She and the others in her unit were trying to help Bihari refugees in the city of Saidpur.

Rosella often wondered how they could help their co-workers, who were Muslims, know Christ as the Son of God. There seemed to be so few opportunities of talking to them about that which was most important in her life.

One day she had an idea. She got a Bible in the Bihari language and put it on a table where people passing by could easily see it. She hoped and prayed that someone might pick it up and start reading it. She tried to keep an eye on that Bible to see what would happen.

In the course of the day she saw many people near the Bible. Some just stood there and talked. Some glanced at the Bible and then walked on. Some were in such a hurry they didn't even see the Bible on the table. They just ran past it.

But one day, when Rosella happened to be in the room, she saw one of the Bihari workers walk over to the table. He was curious. He picked up the Bible. He opened it and started reading! Finally he looked around and when he saw Rosella, he asked, "May I take this book home with me so I can read some more of it?"

"Oh, yes! Of course," Rosella assured him. After he was gone, she immediately placed another Bible in the same place.

A day or two later, the man who had picked up the first Bible, started asking Rosella and the other MCC workers questions about the strange things he had read in it. They answered the questions as best they could but said, "Wouldn't you like to come to our Bible study group? Then we can all search the Scriptures together." The man gladly came.

In time another man picked up the second Bible on the table. He too started asking questions and coming to the Bible study group.

After a while these two Bihari men said they believed in the Lord Jesus Christ but did not want to be baptized until their wives also had become Christians and could be baptized with them.

The two new Christians now organized a Bible study group just for Biharis. More and more people came to it to find out what the Scriptures say.

Rosella Toews was happy. She saw that the Spirit of God was using the Bibles she had placed on the table to bring the good news of Christ to the people.

# 47.
# *The Lion and the Dove*
## *(Vern Preheim)*
## 1976

There had been a long and cruel war in Vietnam. Citizens of the same country fought each other. Some were in favor of the government in South Vietnam. Some were against it and received help from the government of North Vietnam.

The American army and air force, on the side of the South Vietnam government, had burned much of the countryside with its bombs, had destroyed hospitals and schools, and killed many people.

Now the war was over. Christians in North America knew that there was much suffering in Vietnam. There was sickness and hunger. The relief organization called Mennonite Central Committee (MCC) wanted to help the people of Vietnam in the name of Christ. They did not care which side people had been on. They knew that Jesus would want them to help everybody.

In order to find out how they could best help, MCC sent a group of four people to talk with the Vietnamese and decide together with them what would be a good project. Vern Preheim, who was the Asia director for MCC, headed up the delegation.

Vern and the three other MCC workers were welcomed and hosted by the Peace Committee of Vietnam. The people in this committee took them to different places so that they could see for themselves where help was needed most. One of the places where they took them was the spot where the village of My Lai had stood. This village had been wiped out by the Americans. They had burned it and shot down the people as they were fleeing.

The day after the MCC delegation had seen this horrible place, the local committee gave a farewell banquet for them in the city of Da Nang. A project had been decided on. The MCC would re-equip a hospital that had been destroyed during the war. Now it was time to say good-bye.

The host, the highest ranking person at the banquet, was the vice-chairman of the National Liberation Front. He sat across the table from Vern and the two started visiting with each other.

Vern found out that they were the same age and that his oldest child was the same age as the oldest child of his host. His youngest was the same as his host's youngest. There was, however, a big gap between the host's oldest and youngest children because he had been away from home fighting in the hills for twelve years during the war. The host's eyes were friendly. His smiles were warm. Vern felt drawn to him.

Then came the time for the final formalities, which was an exchange of gifts. The host, across from Vern, got up, went to a card table in the corner of the room, and brought back a little lion carved out of marble. The marble had been cut from a hill near the city. The hill, called Marble Hill, had been the place, where, since it contained good hideouts for the Vietcong, some very intense battles between the Americans and the Vietnamese had taken place.

The host held the little lion in his hands as he spoke through an interpreter. He looked straight at Vern. He never glanced away even when the interpreter was talking. Vern did not glance away either. "This lion," said the host, ."symbolizes the courage and the determination of Vietnam in its struggles against the Americans. The lion is strong. He is powerful. We have fought like a lion." The host talked about six or seven minutes and then gave Vern the marble lion as a keepsake.

Now it was Vern's turn. He reached into his pocket and pulled out an MCC spoon. He had not worked out a speech beforehand, but he felt in a very definite way that the Spirit of the Lord was with him and giving him the right words to say at this most unexpected time and place.

Vern held up the spoon and pointed to the MCC logo. "This dove coming off the cross symbolizes our faith," he said. "We are Christians and we have come here on a peace mission. The dove, this bird of peace, penetrates the circle around it. In the same way we have left our circle in North America to come to you on a mission of goodwill."

Vern talked nearly as long as his host. One spoke about a lion, about power and strength. The other spoke about a dove of peace. The whole room was electrified by this brief encounter between the lion and the dove.

Vern handed the spoon to his host. The Vietnamese official was moved. He took the spoon and immediately got up and walked around the table to where Vern was. He gave Vern a strong embrace.

With that all differences melted away. For a moment at least, they were intensely aware that they were both members of the human race, created by God.

# The Good News
## in Japan

# 48.
# *Another Joseph*
## *(Joseph Hardy Neesima)*
## 1843

For many years the country of Japan kept to itself. The leaders would not allow any ships from other countries to land in its ports. They would not allow any of their people to travel to foreign lands.

They were afraid that if they did, people would like the ways of foreigners and lose the culture that was their own. They were afraid that other countries might even fight Japan and conquer it.

It was during that time, in the year 1843, that a boy was born to a wealthy leading family in the city that is now called Tokyo. His name was Neesima Shimeta. Neesima was given special training in the courtesy and etiquette befitting one of his rank. He learned to use the sword. He studied the Chinese classics, which was the mark of a Japanese scholar.

Because Neesima had studied the Chinese language, he could read books written in Chinese by Protestant missionaries to China. This opened a new world to Neesima. He learned there was a country called the United States. He learned about the history of the world.

But most important of all, he learned about the Christian faith. Neesima was a thoughtful boy. He came to believe in God.

But Neesima wanted to know more. He wanted to go to the United States to study and then help his people also learn about God. Unfortunately, even though by now Japan had allowed the first foreign ship to land on its shores, it was still against the law to go to a foreign country.

But Neesima was determined. When he was twenty-one years old he left home without his parents' consent. He went to a northern port and stole aboard an American ship.

When he heard Japanese officers coming aboard to search for any Japanese who might be on the ship, he shook with fear. They were coming closer and closer. Now they were standing a few feet from where he was hiding. Neesima held his breath. If they looked behind the big box they would see him. But they walked on, and Neesima was safe. He was on his way to America.

When the ship docked in Hong Kong, Neesima sold his sword and bought a Chinese New Testament. He could not understand everything he read—it was so strange to him—but he was deeply moved when he read the sixteenth verse of the third chapter of John: "For God so loved the world that he gave his only Son, that whoever believes in him should not perish but have eternal life."

When Neesima came to Boston he was stranded. He had no money. How could he get an education and go back to Japan to help his people learn about God? But Neesima was learning to pray to God as his heavenly Father. And God had a way.

A man by name of Alpheus Hardy was the owner of the ship on which Neesima had come to America. Mr. Hardy heard about Neesima and his desire to study. Alpheus Hardy had wanted to become a minister when he was a young man. Because of ill health he had had to give up that plan and had gone into business. But he wanted to use any money he made in God's service. So he was glad to pay Neesima's way through school.

On board the ship Neesima had been given the name *Jo*. Mr. Hardy thought the name was very fitting. He hoped Neesima would become another Joseph, appointed by God to save his people. In gratitude to Mr. Hardy for his help, Neesima added the name *Hardy* to his name.

While Neesima was in America he was baptized and made plans to return to Japan as a Christian missionary.

At last the time for which Neesima had been waiting so long had come. He went home to his country and his people to help them know God. His family was reconciled to him. He persuaded his father and immediate family to give up their old gods.

He preached in many villages and started a school of higher learning to train leaders. Christian churches came into being.

Even though there was much opposition, Joseph Neesima Hardy kept on working to make his dream come true.

# 49
# *He Cast His Lot with the Poor*
## *(Toyohiko Kagawa)*
## 1909

When young Toyohiko Kagawa of Japan first heard the good news about Jesus from a missionary, he was thrilled. At last he had found someone who was concerned with the sick, the poor, the helpless. Toyohiko Kagawa wanted to follow the Savior who loved all people so much that he died for them. He wanted to live the way Jesus wanted him to live.

As he looked around him, Kagawa saw more and more people who needed help. Right on the seminary campus, where Kagawa was studying to be a minister, he came across a homeless family huddled in a little shed trying to keep warm. They had hardly anything to eat. When a friend made a new kimona for Kagawa, he promptly took it to the poor family to help them keep warm.

After some time Toyohiko Kagawa went to another Christian seminary in the city of Kobe to study. In Kobe there was a bridge crossing the River Ikuta. When you crossed the bridge you came to the worst slums in all Japan.

Kagawa was horrified when he saw how the people lived there, ragged and half-starved, crowded together like animals in filthy little shelters. He preached to them on the street corner that God is love, but how could they believe him when they had to continue living in their misery?

Each evening when he returned from the slums to his comfortable room in the dormitory, he was haunted by the faces of the people across the bridge. He remembered the dirty children watching him wistfully with their dark eyes. He thought of the old people, stooped over with expressions of hopeless despair on their faces. In his mind he again saw the thieves, the outcasts, and the drunkards who lived there. Was there no one in the Church of Jesus Christ who would have compassion on them and go and help them?

Finally, Toyohiko Kagawa decided he could not wait until he had finished school. He was not content just to preach the good news of Jesus Christ from the pulpit—he knew he also had to *be* the good news to these people. In order to be able to do that, he decided to go and live among them.

So it was, that on Christmas Eve of the year 1909, on the night when people think of how the

Son of God came to live among the poor of the earth, Toyohiko Kagawa went to live in the slums of Kobe.

He moved into a little house that was supposed to be haunted because someone had committed suicide there. No one had lived in it for years. An ex-convict, who had listened to Kagawa's preaching, told him about it and helped him carry in his things.

Now Kagawa felt he was where he belonged. He had cast his lot with the poor in order to help them in the name of Christ. He worked with the drunkards, gamblers, thieves, and murderers who were now his neighbors. He started a Sunday school for the children and planned parties for them. He cared for the sick, the homeless, the unemployed. He loved them all because Christ had loved him.

Today Kagawa is known and respected all over the world as the greatest spiritual leader of Japan.

# 50.
# The Tidal Wave

Hamaguchi and his grandson Takahashi were tending the garden in front of their little hut.

"Tomorrow we can harvest our rice," Grandfather announced as he looked proudly at the beautiful rice field nearby. "It is ripe."

Then both of them stopped for a moment in their work to look down at the fertile coastal plain below. From where they stood they could clearly see the little village below them, where at that moment the villagers were celebrating their rice festival.

As was his habit, the old man let his eyes sweep over the gray waters of the Pacific Ocean and on to the distant horizon.

Suddenly he shouted, "Takahashi, quick, fetch me a firebrand from the stove! Quick, quick, my boy!"

Takahashi rushed into the house and brought a burning stick from the stove. The old man snatched it from the boy's hand and ran into his rice field, lighting fires wherever he went. Soon the whole field was ablaze.

"Grandfather, stop it! Stop it!" the little boy screamed. "Why are you destroying our beautiful rice field?"

At the same time, screams came from the village below. "Fire! Fire!" The people had seen the burning rice field and came scrambling up the embankment to Hamaguchi's hillside farm.

The old man pointed toward the ocean.

As the people turned around, they saw a giant tidal wave wash over the plain where a moment ago they had been dancing and singing. All their houses were swept with it.

They stood aghast.

Suddenly someone shouted, "Hamaguchi has saved our lives!" Then others, too, shouted, "Yes, Hamaguchi has saved our lives."

They all fell on their faces and thanked the God of heaven for their neighbor who had not hesitated to sacrifice his rice field to bring them to safety.

# 51.
# *The Shining Village*
## Around 1940

Something amazing and unexpected had happened in the little village of Shimmabuko on the Island of Okinawa. An American missionary on his way to Japan had stopped there and had given a Bible to Shosei and his brother Mojon. He had told them about a loving heavenly Father who cared for them and who had sent them his Son, Jesus Christ, to help them.

"Here is a book which will tell you more about Jesus," he had said before he continued on his way.

Now Shosei and Mojon held this strange book in their hands. Mojon turned the pages to the story of Jesus which the missionary had marked. He read aloud.

"This is amazing," he said. "This book will show us how to live. Look, here it says that we are to love and serve one another."

A crippled man came down the dirty village street. The brothers knew that he had a hard time making a living. He could go fishing only if someone helped him.

"Let us take Crooked Leg with us when we go fishing," suggested Shosei. "That would be helping others as the book says."

Crooked Leg was amazed at being asked. Usually he had to beg to go along. The brothers even shared their lunch with him.

When they came back, Crooked Leg asked the brothers, "Why have you done this for me?"

"It is because of a new teaching we have received," said Shosei. "We have heard there is a loving God who is like a father to us. He wishes us to do good and not evil. He sent his Son, Jesus Christ, to earth to save us from our sins. Would you like to learn more about him, too?"

"Oh, yes!" said Crooked Leg. Day after day he and several others came to sit about the door of the hut where Shosei lived. They listened to the reading from the Bible.

More and more people came to listen. More and more decided to follow Christ and try to live according to his teaching.

That brought about many changes in the village. The people suddenly saw that the roof of the house where a widow lived with her children was leaking badly. They fixed it for her. But now the new roof made the others look shabby so one after another the roofs on the other houses were fixed too.

Mojon studied the Bible more than anyone else and so the people came to him for advice. When someone was angry with his brother, Mojon said, "Forgive him. That is what Jesus said we should do." To the one who had offended, he said, "Do not make your brother angry anymore. Be kind to him."

In time the people of the little village chose Shosei as the new headman. Shosei was careful to make each decision according to the teachings he found in the Bible.

Gradually the old ways of doing things were left behind. Christian ways took their place. Laughter rang out in the village streets, and poverty disappeared when people were fair to each other and lived for the good of all.

The houses were made neat and clean, and the rubbish disappeared from the village streets. Sickness was less common. Rules were made so people could live in peace. The village was happy and prosperous.

Thirty years went slowly by. Shosei and Mojon became old men and were much respected in their villages.

Then another unexpected happening shook the village. A terrible war came to the Pacific. American troops stormed ashore on Okinawa. They forced their way across the island. The village of Shimmabuko lay right in their path. The American troops advanced toward it, bayonets ready, guns leveled. Shosei and Mojon knew they must do something to explain that they were not enemies.

The two little old men stepped forward into plain sight. They smiled and bowed low in front of the soldiers. They spoke words of welcome.

The soldiers halted in amazement. An interpreter rushed forward to hear what Shosei and Mojon had to say.

When he came back, he scratched his head in puzzlement. He told the soldiers, "They are welcoming you as fellow Christians! They say their missionary was an American, and they are overjoyed to see you!"

This was very strange. The officers asked whether they could walk through the village.

The two old men bowed and led the way. The people came out of their houses smiling as if to greet their new friends.

The officers could hardly believe their eyes.

Here was a shining, clean village instead of the dirty, hopeless ones they had seen before. The people were intelligent, healthy, and friendly.

"Tell us," asked one of the men, "how did it happen that you have this kind of a village?"

Mojon told them about the missionary and the Bible he had left with them. He described how the people had studied it and found it its pages a pattern for living.

The officers were silent. They did not know what to say. Before they left the village, Shosei and Mojon showed them the old, old Bible that had made such a difference in their lives.

Then the Americans strode off to their camp. "Maybe," muttered one tough army sergeant, "we have been using the wrong kind of weapons to change the world!"

# 52.
# *Pray Without Ceasing*
## Around 1970

Young Sano was a paperboy in Japan. He had just experienced the great joy of accepting Christ as his Savior and Lord.

Everything was new to him, so he also wanted a new name. He was a quiet boy by nature, so he wanted to be called *Andrew.* He felt that the Apostle Andrew must have been a bit shy and not so outgoing as his brother Peter.

The Andrew in Japan took his Christian faith very seriously. He faithfully attended the Bible study meetings and tried to learn as much as possible.

At one time the group was discussing the verse "Pray without ceasing," (1 Thess. 5:17).

"What does that mean—without ceasing?" asked Andrew.

"I think it means we should pray all the time, "said one of the others in the group.

Andrew could not quite understand how that was possible, but he decided to try it.

The next morning, early, he took his bag of papers. He got on his bicycle and started pedaling. Then he closed his eyes and prayed. The next moment, wham, crash, he landed in the ditch!

Slowly Andrew got up. He got back on his bicycle and started pedaling—this time with his eyes open. He realized he had a lot to learn about the Christian faith.

Andrew did learn. Today he is a pastor in one of the Christian churches in Japan. He now knows that you can live the Christian life with your eyes wide open.

# 53.
# *What Is Poor?*

It was the first day of the New Year. Large snowflakes were falling softly on the pine trees and bamboo branches in the narrow streets of a little town in Japan. Little Aiko was hurrying home through all this wonderland, but she did not see it. She was crying.

Finally she reached home. She pushed back the sliding door, stepped out of her shoes and took off her coat. Then she bowed to her mother and burst out, "What is poor, Mother? The girls at the park say we are poor. Are we, Mother?"

Mrs. Ogawa looked up from her sewing. She shook her head, "No, Aiko, we are not poor."

"What is poor?" asked Aiko again.

"Poor means having nothing to give away to others," said her mother.

"Oh! " Aiko thought about that. She looked around the room. It was the only one they had and there was very little in it. She thought about the things that were hers. She had a cloth schoolbag and several books, but she needed those. She had some clothes, but she could not give those away.

"I guess I am' poor, Mother," she said at last. "I have nothing to give away- it

"Everyone has something to give," said her mother. "You think about it and you will find something."

Aiko sat down on the "tatami" that covered the floor and started gluing hair on one of the dolls that her mother was making to earn a living for her family.

As she worked, Aiko thought again of how it had been when her father was still living. He had told many stories.

"Stories!" cried Aiko. "I can tell stories, Mother! I can give them to my friends."

Mother smiled. "That is a good idea, Aiko. You are a good storyteller just like your father was, and everyone likes stories."

"I am going to start giving them away right away," said Aiko.

She dressed warmly and ran out of the house. Across the street her brother Toru and his friend were playing in the snow.

"Toru! Sano!" called Aiko. "Come here. I have something to give you."

The boys came running. It was New Year's Day. They thought Aiko might have a treat for them.

"What is it?" they asked.

"Sit down on the bench," said Aiko. "I have some stories to tell you."

"Oh, stories," said Toru in disgust. "I have heard all your stories. Come on, Sano, let's go and play."

Aiko tried to force Toru to sit down. "You must stay. I want to give you stories. I have a new one you haven't heard."

But Toru and Sano just ran away and laughed.

Sadly Aiko went back into the house. "I wanted to give Toru and Sano a story, and they wouldn't listen, Mother," she said.

"We should not force our gifts on people," said her mother. "Gifts are only for people who want them."

"Toru did not want my gift," said Aiko. "I had a new story. It is the one about Joseph and his jealous brothers. I heard it in Sunday school when Toru was home with a cold."

"That is a very good story," said her mother. "It ends in forgiveness."

Later on the little family sat down to their New Year's meal. They all bowed their heads and Mother thanked their heavenly Father for his help during the past year and asked him for his guidance during the next. Then they ate. It was a good supper.

After the dishes were washed, Toru said, "Mother, please tell us a story."

"Aiko is the best storyteller in our family," she said. "She wanted to give you a story, Toru."

Toru looked down. Then he said. "Please, Aiko, tell me the new story you have."

Aiko smiled. They all settled down and she told them the story of Joseph.

"That is a good story," said Toru. "Joseph was a tattletale but he grew up to be a man that didn't hold a grudge. Will you tell the story to Sano tomorrow?"

"Of course," said Aiko happily.

She knew now that she was not poor. She had a gift to give. It was a good way to start the new year.

# 54.
# *We Are Ready to Go*
## *(Masaki and Shiori Yamazaki)*
## Around 1980

Sunday was a very special day for Masaki and Shiori Yamazaki and their three little boys. That was the day they all got ready to go to the Obihiro Japanese Mennonite Church to worship. It took them a whole hour to get there, so they had to start early.

One Sunday there was a surprise at church. A man from the Mennonite Central Committee told the boys and girls and the men and women in the congregation about the people in Bangladesh.

He said the people there did not have enough to eat.

He said they needed someone to show them how to grow better crops.

He said they needed someone to show and tell them that God loved them and cared about them. The Yamazaki family listened carefully.

When the man was gone, the people in the Obihiro congregation looked at each other. "Can we help?" they asked.

"We could give some money," someone suggested.

"Maybe we should do more than that," someone else said. "Missionaries have come to us here in Japan to tell us about Christ. Perhaps we should now send someone to Bangladesh to tell them the good news and help them."

It was a new thought. The people got excited. "But who would go? It would have to be a very special person who knows all about the land and growing crops."

Immediately all the people looked at Masaki Yamazaki.

"Why, Masaki, you are the very one!" they exclaimed. "You teach agriculture. You could help them."

Then someone added, "And, Shiori, you are a good youth leader. You could work with young people in Bangladesh."

It was quiet a bit and then they asked, "Masaki and Shiori, we can't all go. Will you go for us? We will give money to pay for your trip."

Masaki looked at Shiori. Shiori looked at their three little boys. Then Masaki and Shiori shook their heads a little bit. "We don't know," they said. "We will need to think and pray about it."

"And we will all pray with you so that God might lead us to do his will," said the people in the congregation.

When the Yamazaki family drove home that Sunday they were very much excited.

"Maybe God is calling us to do this," said

Masaki. "I would like to help the people in Bangladesh."

"But how can we take our three little boys so far away from home?" asked Shiori.

"We will be good," said one of the little boys.

"We will play with the little children in Bangladesh and give them some of our food," said another.

"And I will tell them stories," said the littlest one. "I know about Jesus and the children."

Their father and mother smiled.

Not very long afterwards Masaki and Shiori Yamazaki and their three little boys told the congregation at the Obihiro Church that they were ready to go to Bangladesh under the Mennonite Central Committee.

There was great rejoicing in the church at the news, and one Sunday they had a farewell for the Yamazaki family. Masaki and Shiori knelt down and while the pastor prayed that God might bless them, the people of the congregation came and laid their hands on them. They wanted to show the whole family that they would not forget them. They would pray for them and support them.

Masaki spoke for the whole family when he said, "We are going to Bangladesh because we love Christ and we want to do everything in his name."

# The Good News
# in Taiwan

# 55.
# *Mother of the Taiwan Tribes Church*
## (Chi-o-ang)
## Around 1940

The people of the Tyal tribe in the mountains of Taiwan had never heard the good news that Jesus loved them. There was no Bible in the language of the Tyal people. The missionaries in Taiwan, who knew only Chinese, could not speak to them.

But God had prepared a way. Years ago a girl of the Tyal tribe had married a Chinese merchant in the plains. Her name was Chi-o-ang. She soon learned the Chinese language. She read the Chinese Bible. In time Chi-o-ang became a Christian.

The missionaries heard about Chi-o-ang. They went to her and said, "You know both Tyal and Chinese. Come to our Bible school and learn how to tell the story of Jesus to the Tyal people."

Chi-o-ang was middle-aged and frail by this time. But she felt this was a call from God. She went to school for two years. Then she went up into the mountains that were home to her and began to teach. She went from village to village. The people loved and respected Chi-o-ang and began to listen to the gospel. Many of them became Christians.

But then trouble came. The Japanese had conquered the Island of Taiwan. They wanted all the people to speak Japanese and they wanted all the people to believe in the Shinto religion. They came to Chi-o-ang and said, "You are teaching the religion of another nation. It is not permitted. You must stop going from village to village and telling the people about Christ."

Chi-o-ang was not allowed to travel anymore. But the men and women, boys and girls, who had heard her, wanted to know more about Jesus. If Chi-o-ang could not come to them, they decided to come to her.

Late at night, one at a time, they would come and slip into her house. Sometimes a man would walk twenty miles from his village and after an hour or two of listening, he would leave and reach home before dawn. Even though they were very careful, the Japanese still suspected something was going on. But Chi-o-ang did not care. She knew she was doing what God wanted her to do.

One day she said, "I must go to the village of Mikasa Yama. The followers of Jesus there need to be encouraged."

"No, no!" cried her friends. "It is too dangerous. The Japanese are watching for you."

But danger never stopped Chi-o-ang. She took the train and got off at the station nearest to the village where she was going. The Christians there were delighted to see her. Quickly they gathered in one of the houses for worship.

But suddenly they heard the sound of a trumpet. It was the warning signal.

"The police! They will search for you," cried the people.

"Come, beloved grandmother, we will hide you in the hills" said the young men.

"I am too old," said Chi-o-ang. "No longer can I climb the rocky paths."

A sturdy young man took her on his back. She was small and thin and frail. "We will take turns carrying you," said several others. Away they went.

They reached a village higher up in the mountains. The Christians there welcomed her with tears of joy, but they said, "Chi-o-ang, it is not safe for you here."

After a little rest the young men took her to the next village.

There, too, the Christians were overjoyed to see her. But they said, "Oh, Chi-o-ang, the

Japanese have telephoned to this village that you are in the hills. The police have orders to search every house."

As the police began to search one end of the village, Chi-o-ang and the young men slipped out the other end. The men carried the tired old woman tenderly. They took Chi-o-ang to a train station and were able to get her on a train going to her home village without the police seeing her.

The train rolled away into the darkness. But at the next station, six men got on to search for Chi-o-ang. A young man, also getting on the train, who was a Christian, saw them. He pushed into the train ahead of them and raced through the cars until he saw Chi-o-ang.

"You are my baggage," he said. He spread out a big cloth he had with him. Chi-o-ang curled up on it on the seat, and he tied her up in the cloth like a bundle of clothes. He sat down beside her. When the searchers came by, they walked right past her. Chi-o-ang reached home in safety.

As the days went by, Chi-o-ang continued to teach and comfort and support the Christians who suffered much persecution.

Finally the war was over and the Japanese had to leave the island. The Christians were safe. Down to the churches in the lowlands came the secret Tyal believers. They joined the Christians there and asked for baptism.

After the war the missionaries came back to Taiwan. They found to their amazement more than four thousand Tyal people who had become Christians through the faithful service of Chi-o-ang.

# 56.
# *A God of Love*
## (Mary Gau)
## Around 1945

Far away in a village in the rugged mountains of Taiwan there lived a little girl called Gau Fu-Mei.

One night Fu-Mei had a strange dream. It was so clear and so real that when she woke up she knew exactly what she had dreamed. In her dream she was told that there was a God who loved her.

Fu-Mei was amazed. She had never heard of such a thing. The gods in which her people believed certainly did not love people. Her people believed the gods were angry and hated them. Fu-Mei was afraid of the gods.

But now through her dream, she knew there was a God who loved her. She was so excited that she told everyone. Soon all the people in her village knew about her dream. Most of them paid little attention to it, but some said, "Fu-Mei, don't talk about a God of love. Our gods will be angry and something terrible will happen."

Very soon after the dream Gau Fu-Mei's father became ill and died. "See," said the people in her village, "the gods are punishing you for your chatter about a God who loves you."

Fu-Mei was sad. Then she became frightened because her younger brother also became very ill. What if he should die? Then most certainly people would say it was Fu-Mei's fault.

Fu-Mei could not sleep. Quietly she slipped out of the house at night so she could see the stars. Somehow she felt closer to this unknown

God there. She pled with him. She said, "If you are really the God I think you are, please take away my little brother's sickness."

The next morning, the little boy's fever dropped and soon he was well again.

Fu-Mei was so happy her heart almost burst. God had answered her. There was something to her dream. There really was a God of love.

But she wanted to know more about this God. She wondered how she could find out. Were there other people who knew about him?

When Gau Fu-Mei was old enough, she went to a big city on the coast to work. Perhaps here she would meet someone who knew God. But Fu-Mei was shy, so she did not ask. And the people with whom she worked were not kind. They could not possibly know much about a God who loves, she thought. Disappointed Gau Fu-Mei returned home again.

After some time an evangelist came through her village. When he met Fu-Mei, he said, "Aren't you the girl who wants to know more about Christianity?"

"Yes, yes!" said Fu-Mei eagerly.

"Then go to the Mennonite Christian Hospital in the city of Hwalien. The people there teach about the God of love."

Fu-Mei was soon on her way to Hwalien. She decided to enter the school of nursing at the hospital the evangelist had mentioned. Then surely she would hear something about this mysterious God who had talked to her in her dream so long ago.

When she came to the hospital to apply, she saw about sixty other girls there who wanted to enter the nursing program. It was frightening. They all had to write entrance exams and Gau Fu-Mei didn't know the answers to most of the questions. How could she when she had not been able to go to school very long? Her heart sank. Would the people in charge of the hospital let her stay? Would they not be kind? But if the people here knew the God of love, maybe they would understand.

The next morning several people interviewed her. Sue Martens, the missionary nursing instructor, looked at her with loving eyes. But she said, "Gau Fu-Mei, it seems to me you would have a great deal of difficulty keeping up with all the studying in the nursing program, because you do not have enough schooling. Why do you want to become a nurse?"

Gau Fu-Mei was too shy to talk about the real reason. She just said over and over again, "Please let me stay. Please let me stay. Please let me study here. I will work very hard."

Finally the hospital committee decided to let her try the nursing program for a while. Gau Fu-Mei, or Mary Gau as she was called at the hospital, was jubilant.

Her nursing instructor was kind. The doctors were kind. They all seemed to have something different about them. She soon found out why. They were trying to live like Jesus Christ, the Son of the God of love. They told her about him. They taught her that Jesus had died for her sins and that she could come to God without fear.

After two years, Mary Gau came to Sue Martens and said, "I now have what I came for. I have reached my goal. I will return to my village."

"But why do you want to quit now?" asked Sue. "You are doing well and you have only one more year to go until you are a nurse!"

"No," smiled Mary Gau shyly. "I came to learn about a God of love I dreamed of when I was a child. In these two years I have learned to know him. He is truly all I hoped he would be. I have taken his Son as my personal Savior. Now I want to return to my home village and share the good news of God's love with the people there."

That is what Mary Gau did. She went home to her village. In time she was married. She and her husband now serve a Christian church close to their home, and in word and deed share the love of God which they have experienced.

# 57.
# *The Golden Ring*
## Around 1960

Mrs. Yang was a little old lady in Taiwan. She had been a Christian for a long time and now finally she also had found a group of other Christians with whom she could worship. Every Sunday she walked for a whole hour to get to the little Mennonite Church in Hsitun. She could hardly wait for Sunday to come around, she enjoyed going to church so much.

For several Sundays now, however, when she walked to church, she knew there would be no little church in which they could gather for worship. A great flood had raged through the village and had swept away many homes as well as the church. They now met in a little fuel shed which had been left standing.

All the people crowded into the shed. It was far too small. They knew they needed to build a new church. But how could they? Most of the people were older, like Mrs. Yang. Many of their homes had been damaged by the flood. There was no money.

Mr. Ong, their minister, encouraged them to pray. He told them that if they could gather some money and would help with the work of building the chapel, the other Mennonite churches in Taiwan and in America would help them.

While Mrs. Yang was sitting in the little shed, she kept thinking, "How I wish I could do something to help build a chapel. I have time, but I am too old to help with the work of building, and I have no money. I have nothing to sell. There is nothing I can do."

Her heart sank. Then her eyes fell on her ring. It meant very much to her. It had been a wedding gift from her husband.

"This ring is very old," she murmured softly, "but it is made of gold."

Slowly she slipped it off her finger.

At the close of the service she walked quietly to the pastor, pressed the ring into his hand, and said, "This is the only thing I have that is of any value. I want to give it to the Lord. Please take it and use it to build our own chapel."

Pastor Ong's eyes grew moist as he saw the golden ring. He rejoiced that this woman was willing to give her most prized possession to God.

Many other people also gave of the little they had. Those who could helped with the building, and so in about half a year a new chapel was dedicated to the Lord in Hsitun. Mrs. Yang and many others were there to praise God for this house of worship.

# The Good News
# in Africa

# 58.
# *Opening the Way*
## (David and Mary Livingstone)
## 1813-1873

David Livingstone, the missionary in Africa, had a big dream. He and his wife Mary and their children, Robert, Agnes, and Baby Thomas, were living in a little house in southern Africa where they taught the African people about the love of Christ. But David was always thinking about the vast regions to the north where no missionary had ever gone. He dreamed of opening a way for the gospel among those tribes who had never heard of Jesus.

One day the whole family set out in a wagon on the long journey to the country of Chief Sebituane. A number of their African friends accompanied them. They hoped they could start a new mission settlement there. They traveled 870 miles.

On and on they traveled across the endless desert. Often they did not have enough food. Friendly Africans brought the children large caterpillars, a frog, or a locust to eat. The Africans thought they were special treats. Robert and Agnes, who had been born in Africa, liked them very much.

Finally they had crossed the desert and reached beautiful Lake Ngami. On the shore of the lake, David lifted the children from the wagon. They shouted with delight. They raced to the water and paddled and played in it. Their mother and father stood side by side, watching them. How grateful they were to God that he had brought them safely this far!

That night two of the children were burning with fever and some of the African helpers were also sick. The lake was beautiful, but apparently very unhealthy. The whole party had to return home.

A year later they set off again. This time it was even worse. Their guide lost his way in the desert. They could not find any water.

"Mary," said David, "we must use the water we have in the wagon very sparingly until we get to a place where we can get more."

Mary became pale. She said, "The cask in which we carry the water has leaked. There is no water left."

The children were crying because they were so hot and thirsty. Their parents were frightened. If they did not reach water soon, their children would die. They cried to God in their anguish.

Finally, after struggling along for a whole day, one of the men, who had gone ahead, shouted loudly. He had found a little mudhole. The water was dirty, but it saved their lives.

This time they did reach the country of Chief Sebituane, but Mary and the children became so ill with fever that they could not stay there. Once more they had to return to their mission station.

What should they do? David felt God wanted him to go into the interior. They both knew that white slave traders were brutally dragging men and women and children away as slaves and burning their villages. The country must be explored and opened to honest trade, so that slave traders could not do their horrible work in secrecy anymore.

After much thought and prayer, they decided that Mary and the children should go to David's home in Scotland for some time. David would go even farther into the heart of Africa to open the way for further mission work.

That was a hard decision to make. They would be very lonesome for each other—Mary and the children in faraway Scotland, and David on his dangerous trips in Africa.

The slave traders hated David. They knew he would tell the whole world what they were doing. They were determined to stop him. Besides many Africans thought all white men were slave traders who wanted to do them harm. They also wanted to stop him. Another danger was malaria. Often David became very ill.

In spite of all these dangers, David plodded on in his effort to explore Africa, to stop the slave trade, and to spread the good news of Jesus Christ.

Many years went by. David made many discoveries. All the world finally knew about him and honored him. But David was still traveling through the great country of Africa. Starving, in rags, worn out with fever and wasted with sickness, he and a few companions finally arrived at a place where they thought they would find help. But the slave traders were watching for him. They stopped all letters and messages for help. They wanted to see him die. But they had not reckoned with the fact that David Livingstone had many friends.

One day a companion who was with David came to him where he was lying sick in bed, and said, "A white man is coming up country!"

Who could it be? David rose shakily to his feet. A group of men were approaching. A white man came forward. He grasped David's hand.

"Dr. Livingstone, I presume?"

"Yes."

"My name is Stanley," said the man. "I thank God, Doctor, that I have been permitted to find you."

People in America who appreciated the fact that David Livingstone wanted the slaves in America as well as in Africa freed, had been worried that no one had heard anything of David Livingstone for years. So the owner of a paper sent his best reporter out to find him. Stanley was that reporter.

Now finally David heard about the outside world again.

Finally he could send reports of his explorations and discoveries back to Great Britain.

Finally he could tell the whole world about the horrors of the slave trade.

just as he had almost given up hope, his life was spared. He could again go on with renewed strength.

Long after both Mary and David Livingstone had died and their children were grown up, it became clear how their efforts had paved the way for the good news of Jesus Christ to spread through the whole continent of Africa. Roads were built, missionaries could come in, and the slave trade was stopped.

At a place where David Livingstone had once stood grieving because of all the people who had been killed by the slave traders, there is now a great mission station called Livingstonia. It is a memorial to the man who made it his life's dream to open Africa to the good news of Jesus Christ and his love.

# 59.
# *Singing the Bible*

Even though it was very hot, the people in a little church in Africa liked to sing. They sang one hymn after another.

Mr. and Mrs. James, the missionaries, who were visiting the little congregation, easily recognized the words and the tunes. They were all songs that had been translated from hymns in America and were now being sung to the same tunes. They did not sound at all like African music.

After the service, Mr. James asked one of the evangelists, "Do you not have any hymns that are African?"

Evangelist Abraham shook his head, "No, we have no songs that could be used in Christian worship."

The other evangelists also shook their heads. They were all a bit shocked. Their own African chants? No, they were not suitable.

Mr. and Mrs. James were disappointed. Everywhere they went, they asked the same question, but no one had any African songs that could be sung in church.

After some time Mr. and Mrs. James again came back to the same village where Evangelist Abraham was living and teaching. There were many greetings. Then everyone sat down and talked.

At first the children sat around the edges of the crowd of grown-ups, to listen, but soon they got tired of it. They slipped away and began one of their games. They sang and clapped their hands as they stamped their feet and danced.

Mr. and Mrs. James began to listen.
"I have heard good news today!"
"Oh, who told you?"
"God's messenger!"
"Christian, oh, who told you?"
"God's messenger!"
The children sang on and on.

"Abraham"—Mr. James interrupted the conversation—"Abraham, that is exactly what we have been asking for! There it is! An old, old, African tune, but the words are Christian words."

Evangelist Abraham looked surprised. "Is that what you meant? Why, that is nothing but an old tune that everyone knows. We often make up verses about the Bible stories and fit them to that tune."

Abraham called the children closer.

"Come," he said, "and sing for our guests the verses that tell the story of Jesus blessing the children."

Abraham turned to Mr. and Mrs. James. "The children made up these words themselves," he said proudly.

So the children clapped and stamped and danced with joy as they sang the Bible stories according to the well-loved pattern of their own African songs.

When they had finished and had gone off to play, Evangelist Abraham said thoughtfully, "The children go home and sing the stories while they are playing. People who wouldn't come near our Christian preaching, sometimes come to me privately and ask, "What is this good news about which the children are singing?"

Mr. and Mrs. James were delighted. They had found what they were looking for. When they went back to the mission station, they carried with them the old African tune with its new Christian words. They sang it to the people in the church.

"Why, this is our own music!" cried the listeners delightedly. "This music speaks to our hearts!" And almost at once they could sing the new words.

Then they began to remember other old songs. They began to fit Christian words to the old tunes. But most of all they still love the new-old song that the children in Abraham's village sang:

"I have heard good news today!"
"Oh, who told you?"
"God's messenger!"
"Christian, oh, who told you?"
"God's Messenger!"

And they still love to go on with verse after verse, singing the Bible stories and teachings, telling what God's Word has taught them.

# 60.
# *I See It Coming*

In Hosi's village in Africa, stories were told every night of the week. just as soon as supper was over, Hosi, who was nine, sat outside the door of his little round home to watch and wait.

Soon all around the village, boys and girls and mothers and fathers came out of their houses to wait for the chief. Finally the chief, wearing a red blanket with bells on it, came from his house. He led them all to the *onjango*, a big circle with a round grass roof over it, held up by posts.

A fire burned brightly in the center. Hosi called it "the story fire." The chief sat down on a stool near the fire. Then all the village people sat down around him.

Stories did not come first. To begin with, important matters of the tribe were discussed and taken care of. Sometimes Hosi could hardly wait. But finally, after all the business matters were finished, the chief gave his blanket a mighty shake so that all the bells tinkled loudly. That was the sign that story time could begin. Hosi shivered with excitement.

At first all was quiet. No one knew where the story would come from or who would tell it. Everyone just sat and waited, waited, waited, until ...

"I see it coming!" said one of the men. Those were the exciting words with which a story always began. "I see it coming!"

"Let it come!" shouted all the others.

The man began, "Once there was a terrible drought in all the land."

Hosi wriggled with pleasure. It was the turtle story. His favorite story. He had heard it many times but he wanted to hear it again.

In the next few years Hosi heard the turtle story in the *onjango* many times.

Then a great change came. When Hosi was fourteen, he had a chance to go to school in a village seven miles away. The big school was very strange. Hosi was homesick for the little round hut which was his home. He felt like running away, but one thing kept him at school—stories.

Every evening in the big room the teacher told stories—new stories that Hosi had never heard before—stories about other tribes that didn't live in Africa, but in faraway lands. There was a story about a boy called Joseph, and a story about a boy named David who became king, and a story of Samuel who heard God speak to him.

"That would sound good in the *onjango*, thought Hosi after each story. Sometimes after he had gone to bed he would practice telling a story. "I see it coming!" he would whisper to himself.

Soon Hosi learned that all these stories were written down in a book called the Bible and that the Bible was in his own language. After that Hosi wanted to learn to read. Someday he wanted to tell those stories in the *onjango*.

Hosi studied hard. After he had finished school he went to another school far away to study the Bible more thoroughly.

Years passed before Hosi returned to his village. A new chief was in power who did not know Hosi. The chief was angry that Hosi had come. He was afraid because Hosi could read a book and he could not.

"Do not be afraid of me," said Hosi. "The book I bring speaks of Suku, our God, the creator of heaven and earth. It tells of his love for us."

"I do not want your book," said the chief angrily. "I'll drive you out of the village."

When evening came Hosi sadly went to the *onjango* and sat with all the rest of the people. When the fire was built up and everyone waited for a story, Hosi suddenly knew what he should do. The turtle story would help him.

"I see it coming!" said Hosi.

"Let it come!" shouted the others.

So Hosi began. "Once there was a terrible drought in all the land. First the little streams dried up, and the springs dried up, and even the rivers dried up. The tall grass crackled in the hot wind. Even the jungle was parched and brown. All the animals were very thirsty and many died.

"Then it was that the elephant, great and important chief of the jungle that he was, called a council of all the animals. From all the parts of the jungle they came dragging along, red-eyed and weary and thirsty and cross, to decide what might be done about the terrible drought, and to consult as to where they might find some water.

"The tiger came, and the leopard, and the deer, and the giraffe, and the hippopotamus looking more wrinkled and dusty than ever. The elephant shook his powerful head from side to side, and asked if there was anything that could be done. But all the animals hung their heads in discouragement, for each had been searching far and wide, and none had found water.

"At last the turtle appeared at the council, and crawling into the circle, he said, "O elephant, great chief of the jungle, listen to me, and I will tell you where there is a spring.'

"But the elephant looked with scorn on the turtle. 'Hush, foolish one,' he said, and lifting him on the end of his trunk, he hurled him over his head and far back into the jungle.

"The turtle righted himself and crawled back to the council circle. Again he stood before the chief, and said, 'Great and honorable one, in my travels I have seen the spring. Come with me—' But before he could finish speaking, the elephant again lifted him on his trunk and again threw him far back into the jungle.

"The turtle almost gave up. But when he thought of the fresh water that would give life to all, he decided to try once more, and the third time he appeared, the tiger said, 'O chief, it can do no harm to listen to the turtle. Let us follow him, and if there is a spring, our lives will be saved.'

"Thus it was decided, and all the animals set out in a weary, solemn procession, following the turtle far, far back into the jungle. At last they came to a hole from which bubbled a fresh spring of water. Then every animal drank, for the spring was never dry. After each one had drunk, he turned to the turtle to say, 'Twa-pa-ndu-la, thank you.' And the turtle was happy because he had saved their lives."

Everyone in the *onjango* was glad to hear Hosi tell the old and favorite story. They smiled and clapped their hands softly.

The chief was pleased, too, and a little proud that Hosi belonged to this village and could tell such a good story,

Then Hosi took the Bible in his two hands and held it while he addressed the chief, saying, "O Chief, I have brought a message for my people. Like the spring, it will bring new life to our village. And if you drive me away, I will come back. Like the turtle, I will come back again and again and again."

When the chief saw how earnest Hosi was, he decided that the village must listen, and he said, "We will listen to your message. In the *onjango* we will listen."

Every evening after that, in the *onjango*, Hosi told stories from the Book. All the people listened to him. As they heard the stories over and over, they came to believe that Suku was a God of love. They no longer feared the evil spirits as they had in the past, and all the village came to live in a better, happier way.

# 61.
# *By the Side of the Trail*

Once every week some boys from a Christian high school in Bunumba, West Africa, went out to a little village six miles away to tell the people there about Christ and to worship with them.

Yomba and Sahr, Moni, Tomba, Dudu, and Sute liked walking through the rain forest. It was beautiful. And there were so many things to see. Sometimes they got a glimpse of an elephant or came across some monkeys. Besides, they liked singing as they walked.

One day, as they came close to the village, Yomba stopped short. "What's that beside the trail?" he asked pointing at something.

"Just a pile of rags soaked from being left in the rain," said Moni.

"No," said Yomba. "Look, the rags are moving. There is something alive in them."

Dudu walked ahead to look. "It is a woman," he said.

Quickly they all came closer. The woman hid her face and tried to cover herself with her rags.

"Why don't you go home to the village?" Sahr asked.

The woman raised her two arms. She had no hands—only scarred and ugly stumps. The boys saw that she had the terrible disease of leprosy. Now they knew why she was an outcast from her village, sitting alone by the side of the trail.

The boys didn't know what to say. They didn't know what to do. They just stood there for a minute and then walked on to the village.

As they preached and prayed and sang with the people, they could not forget the sick woman by the side of the trail.

After the service they asked the people about her. The people knew her, but no one would help her.

Quietly the boys walked home. They didn't feel like singing. They did not feel like talking. What they had seen was too terrible.

When they came back to the dormitory, they went to bed. But they could not sleep. When they closed their eyes, they saw the sick old woman alone by the side of the trail in the rainy season—with no shelter, no food, and only a few wet rags for clothing.

When the other boys in the dormitory were asleep, the six who had been on the trail, quietly gathered around Sahr's bed to talk.

"We must make some plan to help that woman," said one of them.

They all agreed. But how? They knew there was no way of taking her to a hospital because a hospital was too far away. The woman could not walk, and they had no car. They talked and talked. Finally they had a plan.

In the middle of the night they tiptoed through the dormitory and knocked at the door of the principal's bedroom. The principal sat up in bed; he rubbed his eyes in surprise, and called, "Come in!"

Sahr told the story of the woman, the others putting in bits he forgot. Then Sahr said, "We have three requests."

"Yes?" encouraged the principal.

"We want a holiday tomorrow to go back to the village and build a *simbeck* of bamboo and palm to shelter her."

"You may have a holiday," agreed the principal immediately.

Sahr continued. "We want to go to the market to buy a piece of cotton cloth and a blanket for her. Among us we have enough money."

"Very good," said the principal. "What is your third request?"

"Each of us will go without a meal a week. We have friends who will give up meals with us. We want to carry the food we save to the woman, two of us every morning and two of us every evening."

"I have another plan," said the principal. "I will tell the cook to put extra rice and yams in the kettle every day and sometimes vegetables and meat. Carrying it to her daily will be your part. That will be a big gift on days when it is hot or rainy. Six miles over an uneven trail is a long walk."

The next day the same boys and a few of their friends walked back along the jungle trail. Some had knives for cutting branches and palm leaves to weave the walls and roof of the shelter that was called a *simbeck.* One carried cloth and another a blanket. Yamba carried a large bowl full of good rice from the school kitchen.

The poor woman was in a daze at first. It was so long since anyone had been kind to her. She ate hungrily. She held the new cloth and the new blanket to her cheek, crooning an old song of her tribe. Then she sat there in wonder as her little shelter took shape.

When the boys left, the little old woman called after them, "May God walk you well!" It was the farewell used in her tribe. "May God walk you well!"

The boys kept their promise. Every morning before school two boys walked from Bunumba to the *simbeck* by the side of the trail, carrying a bowl of food. And every evening after the last class, two other boys walked the same trail with another bowl of food.

A shelter of bamboo and palm does not last forever in a land of rain and insects. After about a year the boys built a new *simbeck.* This time a crowd of villagers gathered to watch them.

"It is strange to see you boys making this *simbeck,*" said one of the men. "The woman's own people did not help her. They put her out in the rain. Then you boys came and cared for her."

The man thought awhile. Then he added, "Only Christian boys would have thought of such a plan. Only Christian boys would have stuck to it and carried it out."

# 62.
# *Free to Fly*

In a village in the faraway country of Angola there lived a little boy called André Mosaki. Little André could not go to school because there was no school in his village, and no one there had ever gone to school.

But André helped his mother in the garden, and he helped her carry vegetables to the market. That was exciting. Very early in the morning when it was still dark, André and his mother would start walking to the town where they could sell their vegetables.

André liked going to market. He liked it especially when his friend came, too. One day while they were at the market André and his playmate each caught a little bird. They tied one end of a string to one foot of the bird and the other end of the string to a twig.

Now André and his friend had a lot of fun. While holding the twig in one hand they would let go of the little bird. The frightened bird would start flying, thinking that at last it was free, only to find itself being jerked back by the string tied around its foot. The boys played with the birds like this for a long time. They let the birds go and then jerked them back. Later they planned to pull off the birds' heads and then roast and eat them.

While they were sitting there playing with the

birds, a long shadow suddenly fell over them. The boys looked up. It was a tall man looking down on them.

"What are you doing?" the man asked.

André and his friend explained the game they had invented.

The man looked at André Then he asked, "Would you sell me your bird?"

André was surprised. What did the man want with the bird? But he said yes immediately.

The man pulled out a five-cent piece from his pocket and gave it to André

André untied the bird and gave it to the man.

For a moment the man held the poor frightened little bird in the hollow of his hand. Then he stretched out his arm high above his head and opened his hand. Away flew the bird into the blue, blue sky. It was free at last!

Now the man turned to André's friend.

"Will you sell me your bird, too?" he asked.

"Yes, oh, yes," said the boy. He was eager to get some money too.

The same thing happened. The man let the little bird fly away after its companion.

The boys were puzzled. They could not understand why anybody would do such a thing.

The man sat down in the dust with them. "Are you wondering why I did this?" he asked.

The boys nodded their heads

"I used to do a lot of bad things," said the man. "I couldn't help myself. It was like being tied to that string. But God sent his Son Jesus into the world. Jesus untied the string. And now I am free like those birds. That is why I gave them their freedom."

André and his little friend could not quite understand what all this meant. But the man was kind. They liked him. The man was an Angolan pastor. He saw to it that André could go to school.

Many years later when André was grown up, he became a writer and a teacher and helped his people in many ways. He always remembered the little incident in the marketplace. Now he understood what his pastor friend had meant when he let the birds fly away.

# 63.
# *They Could Trust Him*
## (Kabangu Thomas)

Pastor Kabangu had a terrible problem. He had faithfully taught the people in his church in Africa about Jesus. But now there was war. The people of the Lulua tribe and the Baluba tribe were fighting each other. Even some members of Pastor Kabangu's church were now enemies. They thought they had to obey their tribal leaders more than they did God.

Pastor Kabangu belonged to the Baluba tribe. He knew his tribesmen wanted him to help them fight the Lulua people.

"You are our relative," they said. "You are tall and strong. You have a better gun than any of the rest of us. You must help us kill the Luluas or else they will rule over us."

"No," said Pastor Kabangu. "It is not my business to fight against flesh and blood. It is my business to fight against evil. That I do with the Bible."

"Then at least give us your gun," they said. "We will protect you with it."

"No," said Pastor Kabangu again. "I can't do that either. I have always used the gun to kill animals for food for my family and for my church members. You would use the gun to kill people. I work for God. He would know. He has given me the work of saving souls. He has not given me the work of destroying bodies. I cannot give you the gun."

Pastor Kabangu's tribal people were very angry.

"Ha," they said. "You must have made friends with the enemies. You are planning to give your gun to them."

"No," said Pastor Kabangu. "It makes no difference who the people are or from which tribe they come. I give my gun to no one."

Finally the men left. Pastor Kabangu quickly hid the gun between the ceiling and the roof where neither tribe could find it and where it would be destroyed if someone should burn the house down.

Soon terrible fighting broke out. One day forty of Pastor Kabangu's tribesmen came to his house again.

"Come and fight with us to protect our loved ones," they demanded.

"No," said Pastor Kabangu again. "I am your pastor. I have baptized many of you. I have dedicated your babies. I will not spill blood on the ground. If I kill somebody it would be taking the place of God and saying, 'Today your life must end; your soul enters eternity.' That I cannot do."

"We have been sent by our chief to get your gun," said the tribesmen. "If you won't give it to us, we will take it by force."

"You are strong enough to take it," said the pastor, "but you will have to kill me first. But even then you would not find the gun."

The tribesmen argued among themselves. Finally they said, "You are no longer a member of our tribe. We will not protect you. The people of the enemy tribe will not protect you." With that they left.

Pastor Kabangu and his family could not sleep. Outside there was shooting and screaming. They could see the red glow of fire People were running from their burning homes.

Pastor Kabangu and his wife knelt down by the bed and prayed. They wept. They waited for the morning. No one came. Again it was night. They knew that people hated each other so much now that someone would come for the gun and probably kill them. They thought it was their last night on earth.

Suddenly there was a knock at the door. So now they had come! Pastor Kabangu slowly went to the door and opened it.

There stood David Kalala, an elder in the church who was of the enemy tribe, but who had not allowed hate to enter his heart.

"My tribesmen are planning to kill you," he said. "I have a truck here. I will take you to safety quickly before they come for you."

Pastor Kabangu and his family were saved. When the war was over, all the people, both from the Lulua and Baluba tribes, respected him for not taking sides. They could trust him as their pastor. He had not helped kill anyone.

# 64.
# A Prepared Path
## (Matthew Kazadi)

The country in Africa that used to be called *the Congo,* had been ruled by white people for a long time. Now independence had come at last and the black people were free. But instead of the happiness and wealth the people had expected, there was quarreling and suspicion and hatred among the different tribes. In fact they were killing each other.

Pastor Matthew Kazadi was very sad. For forty years he had taught the people about Jesus. In the church of Jesus Christ they had all been brothers and sisters. It hadn't mattered to which tribe they belonged. And now suddenly the people had forgotten what Jesus taught because they all wanted more power. Some even hated him, their pastor, because he belonged to a different tribe than they did. A group of armed men, members of his own church, told him to leave or else they would kill him.

What should he do? If he stayed, the people who were of his own tribe would defend him against the others and many would be killed. He didn't want that to happen. If he left, who would help them to love each other again? Who would carry on the work of the church?

"Oh, my God," Matthew Kazadi cried in anguish. "What shall I do? Please show me the way. Tell me what is right. I do not know."

That night Pastor Kazadi had a dream. He saw some women cutting a path through the grass. Others were sweeping it clean. Still others were sprinkling the path with whitewash the way they do in Africa to prepare for an honored guest. Then a voice spoke clearly, "Kazadi, go."

With that Matthew Kazadi awoke. All his burden was gone. He knew now that he must leave immediately. His heavenly Father was preparing a path for him. Surely God would also find a way to take care of the church.

Kazadi and a driver got into a car and drove through the night to another mission station. There they picked up Kazadi's wife and son, who had gone there earlier. Together they started on the way to an airport from which they hoped to be able to leave. It was very dangerous. Everywhere there were people of an enemy tribe who wished to kill Kazadi.

The road was very bad. Sometimes there was hardly a road at all. Finally even the tracks they were following ended. They all got out of the car. They were right at the edge of a river, and there was no bridge across. They could see that at one time there had been a ferry, but now the ferry was deep in the sand. There was no way to cross the river. They could not go forward. They could not go back. It was still night. All they could do was to sit down and wait.

Soon after the sun rose, two men appeared on the other side of the river. They looked surprised when they saw Kazadi and his family.

"What are you doing there?" one of them called.

"We want to cross the river," shouted Kazadi.

"Well, you can't cross it here," the men answered. "The ferry has not worked for a long time. Go back and drive to the place in the river where the ferry crosses. It is about 130 kilometers."

Kazadi did not speak for a while. Then he turned to his family and the driver and said, "We cannot go back. We do not have enough gas and we can't get any more because people are waiting to kill us. We must ask God to help us cross the river here."

"That is impossible," muttered the driver. "The boards of the ferry are all rotten."

But Kazadi prayed. He said, "Dear Father in heaven, you know we are very tired. You know we are in great danger. Don't let us die here. Please find a way for us to cross the river."

Kazadi, his wife and son, and the driver sat down and waited. Everyone was tense. The hours went by.

Finally his wife asked, "Do you still think we are going to get across here?"

"Explain to us how that is going to happen," added the driver crossly.

"I don't know how it is going to happen," answered Kazadi. "I only know that God has prepared a way for us and that he is going to send someone to help us. We will stay right here until that person comes."

They all sat and waited again. It was hot. The insects were bothering them. They were hungry. They were afraid, and angry with each other. No one spoke.

Suddenly they all sat up straight and looked across the river. They saw a young man get into a boat and row across to their side. When he came closer, the young man in the boat cried out in surprise, "Father Matthew Kazadi, is that really you?" It was a former student of Kazadi's who was now working in this part of the country.

Quickly Matthew Kazadi told him their problem. He explained to him that they must get their car across the river here to escape those who were looking for them.

"I'll get some men with shovels from the village to dig out the old ferry and push you across," said the young man immediately and took off on his bike, which he had in his boat.

Before long, twenty men came with their shovels and started digging. They dug out the old ferry. They fixed it. Slowly the car was driven onto the platform, and the men, singing in a rhythmic chant, pushed it across the river.

Matthew Kazadi thanked the men. He prayed that God might help all of them in these hard times.

Then Matthew Kazadi, his family, and the driver continued on their way to safety.

# 65.
# *Famine in the Congo*
## *(Archie Graber)*

Archie Graber, the missionary, was at home in Elkhart, Indiana, on furlough. But he was deeply troubled. He could not go back to Africa because there was too much fighting going on in the Congo where he had been a missionary for many years.

Archie was worried about the people in the Congo. He wondered about his black friends in Charlesville where he had worked. Were they safe? He wondered about all the people who had become Christians. Did they still believe that God could help them when they had to flee from their homes? Did they still love the Lord Jesus Christ when they were hungry and had no place to go? He wanted so much to help them, and there seemed to be no way.

One day Archie was called to come and see the secretary of his mission board. "Some of your friends from Charlesville are refugees now," said the man. "They are asking you to come and help them. The Mennonite Central Committee will pay your way and the Congo

Protestant Relief Agency will put you in charge of bringing food to the refugees and helping them to find homes again. Will you go?"

"Yes," said Archie. I am glad that my friends are asking for me. I feel God is calling me. I am ready to go."

When Archie arrived in the Congo, he could not believe his eyes. There were burned houses. People who had been killed in the fighting lay everywhere. There were homeless people wandering around. There were thousands and thousands of people in refugee camps. They were hungry. The children were crying. There were flies. There was sickness. There was starvation. Over and over again Archie saw people just sitting there, staring straight ahead. They couldn't go anywhere. They were waiting for someone to help them.

But how could he help them? Archie had nothing. Not even five loaves and three fishes like the little boy in the Bible story. Why had God brought him here? He had always been a missionary, calling people to Christ. He had no experience in feeding the hungry. But he knew that he must now show them that God, whom he had taught them to trust, had not forgotten them. Surely God would show him what to do.

God did. God moved the hearts of people in many countries to help. Christians in Switzerland sent money to buy 20,000 blankets. Denmark flew in a plane-load of milk. West German churches sent 700 tents. Belgians shipped 2,000 crates of potatoes. American and European church organizations promised almost half a million dollars in food, medicines, and clothing. United Nations planes started circling over the stricken area like ravens bringing food to Elijah.

Finally Archie Graber and his helpers could start distributing food. At one place, on the first day, 2,000 children each received a vitamin pill and milk. Four thousand people received rice to last one week. Archie Graber went from place to place bringing food and hope and the good news of Jesus Christ.

Many people knew Archie Graber from the days when he was a missionary in their midst. They loved him. They called him *Lutonga*. That meant that they thought of him as a fresh sprout. Now Archie Graber was like a fresh sprout of green to many, many people. There was hope again.

Because he knew the country and the people, the prime minister of that region asked Archie to help to resettle the people in villages. Archie thanked God for this opportunity. At last the homeless people could build homes again.

He and his helpers took a group of people to a place where there was good soil and water. They helped them to erect tent villages at first, and distributed food and Christian literature. They also gave them seeds for planting gardens and hoes to do the work. Later they distributed hundreds of baby chicks so they could in time have meat and eggs.

Archie tried to see that every new village had at least one Christian family in it that could start a church there. Always what was uppermost in his mind was to bring to all the people he met the good news of Jesus Christ.

Archie saw that people were hungry for the Scriptures, so he started a bookstore and a bookmobile in order to sell Bibles. He preached wherever he went. And when he gave food to people he also prayed with them. His black friends knew he was a man of God and their brother.

After several years Archie Graber could go home again. He did not know why God had chosen him for this work, but he was glad that he had had a part in helping his friends.

# 66.
# A Good Samaritan

In the city of Algiers in North Africa there lived some years ago a man by the name of Ahmed. Ahmed had a little grocery store. Every day the people living close by came to buy groceries from him and to pass the time of day. Ahmed was a friend to all.

Hard times were coming to that part of the country, however. Both French and Arab people were living there and they were fighting each other. Ahmed and his neighbors were Arabs and they lived in the Arab part of town. Now the French had cordoned off that area.

Ahmed's neighbors could no longer go out to work. When they could not go to work they no longer had money to buy food. Their children were hungry. They were crying. What should their mothers and fathers do?

Ahmed still had some food in the grocery store. He knew why so few people were coming to buy. At night he could not sleep because he knew his neighbors had gone to bed hungry.

One morning one man came to the grocery store. He looked at Ahmed with sad eyes and said, "I have no money, but could you give me some food if I promise to pay it back later?"

Ahmed looked down. He knew that the man might never be able to pay for the food. But after a moment he said, "Yes, I will give you credit. What do you wish to buy?"

Word spread quickly that Ahmed was selling food on credit.

One by one his neighbors came. Ahmed gave each one something until all the shelves in the grocery store were bare. Then he had to close his store because he had no money left either, but he could now sleep at night. He had done what he could.

# 67.
# A Good Idea

Finally peace had come to Algeria. The fighting between the French and the Arabs had stopped, but the results of the war were still there.

"Look at those hills," said John Carbonare, a Church World Service worker, to his colleagues. "That area has all been burned off by the French military during the war. Since there are no trees there, the soil is eroding. We ought to do something about that."

Vern Preheim, who was the director of both Mennonite Central Committee work and Church World Service in Algeria, looked thoughtful. Then his eyes began to sparkle. A new idea was coming!

"I just received word that the United States is making surplus food available for use as payment for work projects," he said. "You know how much unemployment there is around here. People don't have enough to eat. Let's start a tree-planting project. That will give thousands of people work. We can pay them with food. That way they will get something to eat, and the burned-off hills will be covered with trees again!"

The other workers were excited. Everyone wanted to start planning the project. Vern Preheim wrote letters. John Carbonare talked with people who could help. Soon they got the surplus food. They could start organizing the community and hiring workers.

Nurseries were set up for growing the little trees. Many people were needed to take care of them. Many more were needed to plant the millions of little trees all over the blackened hills.

People were happy. They had food again. And in their hands they were carrying little plants that would once more bring life to their hills.

About five years later Vern Preheim went back to Algeria to the area that had been devastated by the war. He saw a young, beautiful, green forest growing on the hills that had been black before. The erosion had disappeared. And people who had once received food because of the project said they thought the trees were even making a difference in the climate. There was more rain and it was not quite as hot.

Vern Preheim was satisfied.

# 68.
# *Show No Partiality*

*The following story was told by an African minister to illustrate James 2:1-9.*

One Sunday morning, just before the worship service, a poor beggar came to the door of a little church out in the bush. The usher did not really want to let him in. The poor man was in rags and smelled bad. But the usher showed him a seat near the door where the breeze came in so the smell wouldn't be quite as bad.

Soon after the service had started, the poor beggar left, however. The usher was relieved.

A while later another man came to the church. This time the man was dressed in a very sharp-looking Western suit. The usher could tell at a glance that he was a very important man. He bowed to him and took him to the front of the church and got him settled in a good pew.

There was a stir in the church. The congregation did not often have such an important visitor. The minister, who was preaching, got all excited to have such a distinguished visitor in his audience.

After the service the minister and his wife invited the great man to come home with them for dinner. There was a flurry of preparation. Nothing but the best was good enough for the guest.

Finally they all sat down to the meal and the various foods were passed. All eyes were on the visitor of course. He helped himself to the meat, but instead of putting it on his plate, he put it into his pocket. Quickly they all looked away, but they couldn't help realizing how the fat was seeping through the expensive cloth of his suit.

Next came the potatoes. The visitor calmly put them in his other vest pocket. By the time the gravy was passed around everyone was staring open-mouthed at the visitor pouring that into another pocket.

Finally the host could contain himself no longer.

"Sir," he said. "Sir, please, why are you doing this?"

"Well," said the distinguished gentleman, "you obviously did not invite me—you invited my suit. So I am feeding my suit!"

# 69.
# *Working as a Team*

*The following story was told by a minister in East Africa.*

Once upon a time three men were sitting under a tree by a great lake in central Africa. One had the gift of seeing things far away. He said, "I see that my relative on the other side of the bay is very sick. But I have no way to go to see him before he dies."

The second man said, "I have medicine that will heal your relative. But we have no way to get there."

Then the third man, a fisherman, said, I have a canoe. I can help you reach him in time."

They accepted the fisherman's offer. All three crossed the bay in the canoe. They reached the village and gave the sick relative the medicine.

"Now," the preacher asked, "which one of the three cured the man?"

# The Good News
# in Latin America

# 70.
# *Apostle to the West Indies*
## *(Bartolomeo Las Casas)*
## 1492

When Christopher Columbus landed on one of the islands of the West Indies, thereby discovering a new world, he had as a crew member a man by the name of Las Casas. Las Casas could hardly wait until he could go home and tell his young son Bartolomeo about all his adventures.

Bartolomeo was fascinated when his father told him about the storms at sea, about finally sighting land, about his experiences in the new world. Most of all, however, Bartolomeo liked to hear about the people who lived in this new world, people whom his father called *Indians.*

Bartolomeo loved Jesus and he soon felt that he must go to the new world to tell the Indians about the Savior who loved them so much that he died for them. He wanted to help to make the new world a new earth for all.

Ten years after his father had first told him about the Indians, Bartolomeo came to America. Since Columbus had claimed the land for Spain, the Spanish government assigned Bartolomeo some land on which he could live and start his mission work. How amazed Bartolomeo Las Casas was, however, when he discovered that the government had also supplied him with native slaves!

Las Casas was a kind, humble man. He had come to love the Indians. To have them as slaves did not seem right. He took out the Bible he had brought with him. He read on and on. The more he read, the less he could see how, as a Christian, he could possibly own slaves. Christ had died to free all. The Indians were his brothers and sisters—not his slaves.

Las Casas could not preach to the Indians that they were to be free in Christ and still hold them in slavery for his convenience. He let all his slaves go free.

From that time on his life was a continuous struggle to have the Indians treated fairly. He went to Spain to plead with the king and with the head of the church. He pled with people in government.

The people who had no interest in the Indians except to exploit them, hated Las Casas. They opposed him and made life miserable for him. But Las Casas kept on working on behalf of the native people. Finally the government of Spain appointed him protector of the Indians.

Las Casas went to Cuba, Santa Domingo, Puerto Rico, Venezuela, Nicaragua, Guatemala and Mexico. Everywhere he told the Indians about the love of Christ.

Many of the people who had come from Europe were greedy. They just wanted land and gold. They did not care about the Indians. They continued to treat them unfairly and cruelly even when Las Casas tried to protect them.

Bartolomeo Las Casas, who was the first priest ever to be ordained in America, is still called "Apostle to the West Indies."

# 71.
# *Dayuma*

It was a dark starless night in the forest of Ecuador. Inside of the large oval Auca dwelling all the people were fast asleep. All, that is, except Dayuma's mother. She was restless. Somehow she sensed that danger was near. Her clan and a neighboring clan had had a quarrel for a long time. Recently her husband's brother had murdered one of the enemies. What if the dead mans relatives should choose this night to take revenge?

Dayuma's mother stretched out her hand to her daughter. "Dayuma," she whispered, "wake up! Can you hear anything?"

"No," said Dayuma sleepily.

But then they both heard the call of a night bird. That might very well be an imitation used as a signal by prowling Aucas. Quickly they awakened Dayuma's little brother and quietly tiptoed to one of the openings of the building.

But already there was a wild scream. Men from the enemy clan rushed into the house through the opposite opening and started a massacre. Dayuma and her mother and little brother fled into the forest in terror and hid in the bushes.

When it was morning, Dayuma's mother crawled out of her hiding place with her little son. But where was Dayuma? She was not there! Had she run farther into the woods?

Almost all the people in the Auca house were killed. Dayuma's father had died earlier. Dayuma's mother was heartbroken. Day after day she and little brother looked for Dayuma in the forest. Sometimes Dayuma's aunt, Mintaka, went with them. They followed every path they knew. They called her name. But they never got an answer. Dayuma had disappeared.

Some years later something very strange happened. A little plane flew over the large Auca house where Dayuma's mother and brother now lived. They had heard planes before, but this one was different. It seemed to fly very low. No one dared to go out.

But when the plane was gone, they rushed out of the house. There on the path leading to the river was a shiny kettle with a lid! The plane must have dropped it. The men brought it in and Dayuma's mother used it to get water.

A few days later they heard the plane again! This time several men went out to see the plane as it flew low over their heads. And sure enough, there was a line hanging out of the plane and something fastened to it.

Quickly the Auca men ran forward and loosened the gift from the line. It was a machete, a knife that Aucas needed for cutting plants and leaves in the forest. Dayuma's brother touched it. It was sharp. Oh, how he wished he could use it some time!

After that the plane flew regularly over their house and dropped gifts. Sometimes it flew so low that they could see the men in it. They were white men. Nobody was afraid now. Everybody ran out to see the plane. And sometimes after they had taken the gift off the line they tied a gift of their own to it to give to the people in the plane.

The Auca priest frowned. "It is alright to take the gifts and to give gifts," he said, "but remember—if the white men ever set foot in our forest, they must be killed. White people have deceived us too often. They have murdered many of our people. We must take revenge!"

Dayuma's mother shuddered. When would revenge ever end?

The plane kept coming. Always the men in it left a gift, and sometimes when the plane was low enough they could see that the men's faces were very kind. They laughed and waved at the people below and kept calling in the Auca language "Bit miti punimupa." This meant "I like you; I want to be your friend."

Dayuma's mother sighed. Why should they have to kill these men?

One day she said to her son, "These men come from outside of our forest. Perhaps they know something of Dayuma. I wish we could ask them."

The next time the plane came and dangled the cord with the gift on it, Dayuma's brother tried to tie the cord around himself. He waved his arms at the fliers. Couldn't they pick him up so that he could fly away with them to look for Dayuma? But the fliers did not understand and the plane flew off into the distance.

Then one day, the fliers called out different words. The Aucas were puzzled but finally understood them to say, "Come tomorrow to the Curary."

Immediately many of the Auca men set off toward the Curary River to see what was happening there. To their surprise they saw some white men walking around in the river and calling Auca words, saying they would like to be their friends.

When Dayuma's mother heard this she said to her sister Mintaba and her son, "You must go and talk to these men. I am sure they know something about Dayuma."

Mintaba, a friend of hers, and Dayuma's brother set out to find the white men at the river. Sure enough, after walking for several miles, they saw them on the other side of the water.

Dayuma's brother shouted at them and then he and Mintaba and her friend walked out of the forest. The men seemed surprised. Then they shouted, "Puinani!" (Welcome) and began wading across the river to meet them.

They all went back across the river together and the Aucas tried to talk to the white men. But the white men knew only a few Auca words. The Aucas could not make them understand that they were asking about Dayuma. Finally they went home.

The priest saw them coming back to the Auca house. He glared at them. Soon afterwards Dayuma's mother saw a group of men leaving. She knew that they were headed for the white man's tree house and she knew what they were

going to do. No white man that set foot in their forest must be allowed to live. When the Auca men came back, the deed was done. They told the clan how they had killed the five white men.

Dayuma's mother sat with her head bowed. She groaned. So now those kind men were dead. What would their families do? Would they also take revenge? And would she never, never hear from her daughter Dayuma?

But Dayuma's mother never gave up. Several years later, she said to her sister Mintaba and another woman, called Mankamu, "I cannot walk very far anymore, but you can. Please go to the Indian tribe outside of this forest and search for Dayuma there. Perhaps she is living with them."

Mintaba and Mankamu could not say no to Dayuma's mother. They said, "Yes, we will go and come back when the kapoc is ripe." They set out on the long journey on foot. Dayuma's mother looked after them until she could no longer see them in the jungle.

The kapoc was planted and grew and slowly ripened. Every day Dayuma's mother sat on the trail leading into the forest. Some day Mintaba and Mankamu would come back, but would they bring Dayuma with them?

One day she heard footsteps. She looked intently down the path. Yes, someone was coming. Two women? No, there was a third! Dayuma's mother jumped up and ran forward. And the next moment Dayuma and her mother were reunited.

Dayuma had come back. And she had a wonderful story to tell. She had worked for many years with white missionaries to help them learn the Auca language.

"I heard that our Auca men killed five white missionaries," she said. "I will tell you their names. They were Jim Elliot, Nate Saint, Ed McCully, Roger Youderian, and Pete Fleming. I worked with Rachel Saint, Nate's sister, and with Betty Elliot, Jim's wife. I thought they would want to take revenge. But they did not. They told me there is a God who has created all people and loves them all alike—also us Aucas. He loved us so much that He sent us his Son

Jesus Christ to die for the bad things we have done. He forgave us, and he wants us to forgive each other. I now love Jesus, Gods Son, and have become a follower."

"Then revenge has finally ended?" asked Dayuma's mother.

"Yes," said Dayuma. "Revenge has ended for Christians."

"Then I want to hear more about this Jesus Christ," said Dayuma's mother.

Others wanted to hear more too. And so it was that Dayuma, Mankamu, Mintaba, and seven other Aucas set out once more to invite the missionaries to come and teach them about Christ.

Dayuma's mother and the other Aucas built two little thatched huts for them and then waited and waited.

Finally, just like that other time, a group of people came down the forest trail and into the open. This time three white people were with them—Rachel Saint, Betty Elliot and a little girl called Valerie. They had come to bring them the good news that God is love.

# 72.
# *Dona*
## Around 1965

Dona sat on a log in the jungle and stared straight in front of her. She didn't listen anymore. Now she knew that it was true—her family had left her to die in the forest because she had leprosy. At first she had listened and listened. Perhaps they would come back. But all was quiet. There were no footsteps. Only the wind was moaning in the trees.

Dona looked at her hands. They were ugly. Leprosy had shrunk her fingers into stumps. Dona looked at her feet. They too were ugly with leprosy. She hated them. She hated her body. She hated herself. She hated her family for leaving her to die. She hated everyone in the whole wide world. Her hatred grew so big that it was bigger than she. It gripped her and held her sitting there—sitting there—sitting there—as in a vise, waiting for death to come.

But someone else came. She knew horses were walking along the path in the jungle. She knew they stopped in front of her. But she did not look up. She heard the two men on the horses talking to her. "Madam, what is the matter? Why are you sitting there?" But she did not answer. She hated them. She wanted them to leave so she could get on with the business of dying.

But the men did not leave. They talked to her. Finally she felt them lifting her to her feet. She struggled. "Leave me alone," she shouted. "I hate you. I want to die."

The men gently put her on one of the horses and took her many miles to the leprosy station at Kilometer 81. There nurses took care of her. They washed her. They tended her leprosy sores. They gave her food to eat.

Dona could not understand why they were taking care of her when her own family had abandoned her. One day when Dr. John Schmidt, one of the men who found her in the jungle, was giving her medicine, she asked,

"Why do you bother to take care of me?"

"Because God wants us to," Dr. Schmidt said. "He loves you and wants you to live."

Dona thought about that a lot. Did God really love her? Did he really want her to live? The next time the patients gathered for a church service, Dona went too. Maybe she could find out more about God.

Dona learned to love God when she heard how he had sent his only Son to help people with their problems and to tell them what God is like. Finally, after several years, she decided to be baptized to show that she wanted to belong to God's people.

At the baptismal service, she wanted to tell all these people who loved her what had happened to her. She said, "When I was brought from the forest, I hated everyone, including the missionaries who wanted to save me. I could not believe that anybody loved me. I thank you for the help you have given me physically, but much more I thank you for the light of the gospel which you brought to my heart and that I could find my Savior."

# 73.
# *The Search Among Thieves*

Señor Anuncio was a colporteur. It was his business to sell Bibles. He wanted to help as many people as possible to have a copy of the Scriptures, or at least a copy of one of the Gospels. So Señor Anuncio walked steadily down the long country roads of Paraguay, carrying his little suitcase filled with books.

One day he was headed for a small village called Nogales. "Is this Nogales?" he asked a group of children, playing near some houses.

"Yes, Señor "they said.

Señor Anuncio sat down on a log to rest before going on. He smiled at the children standing around him. "Would you like to hear a story?" he asked.

The children crowded closer and sat down on the ground around him. Of course they wanted to hear a story!

"Long, long ago," began Señor Anuncio. He told them one Bible story after another. Always the children begged, "Tell us another."

"Only one more," Señor Anuncio said finally.

This time he told them the story of the selfish son who took his share of his father's money and went away to a faraway place and wasted it all in foolish living.

As Señor Anuncio was telling the story, an old man slowly came up behind him and stood there listening. After the story was finished and the children had run away to play, the old man said sadly to Señor Anuncio, "My son has gone to a faraway place too. He has gone to the big city."

"Tell me about him." said Señor Anuncio.

So the man told him about the boy he loved so much. "His mother and I grieve all day and all night. He left after the sugar harvest, and that is a long time ago."

Señor Anuncio thought to himself, "I will go to the city and try to find that foolish young man."

Instead of walking on as he had planned, Señor Anuncio immediately returned to the city. He went to see some people whose names the old father had mentioned and who were supposed to be friends of his son. From them he found out that the son was keeping company with thieves, but they did not know his exact address.

Señor Anuncio thought and thought. What should he do now? Finally he had an idea. He went to the thieves' part of town and stood on a street corner. There he began telling the story of

**114**

the prodigal son. When he had told it at one street corner, he went on and repeated it at another corner. Sometimes he leaned against a wall in the middle of the block and told the story.

Each time he told it, he thought of the father down in the country, longing for his boy's return. And, thinking of him, he made the story so full of the father's love and desire to see his boy that even the thieves who listened to it were filled with respect.

One dark evening when he had just finished telling the story, a little twist of paper fell at his feet. Someone had dropped it from the window just above him. On it Señor Anuncio read, "Please come up to me." Señor hurried up the dark stairs and knocked on the door of the room whose window had been above him.

In the room was a young man. He said, "I heard your story. It is about a man like me."

"Tell me about yourself," invited Señor Anuncio.

"I lived in a small village named Nogales," began the young man. Señor Anuncio's eyes began to sparkle, but he did not interrupt. "I took all the money I made in the sugar harvest and all my father would lend me, and I came to the city. I thought I would get rich. But I spent the money in foolish ways. My friends helped me spend it, but when I had no money left, they threw me out!"

He bowed his head down in his hands and rocked to and fro. "Stupid, stupid that I was!"

He waited for a moment and then went on, "I was ashamed to go home. My father would be so angry. He might disown me. I thought it was better that he should think I was dead than for me to go home penniless."

Señor Anuncio looked sympathetic, but he asked no questions.

"Tonight," the young man went on, "I heard the story you were telling down there on the street. And the father in the story was not angry. He still loved his son. Do you think," he asked Señor Anuncio, "that there is a chance that my father would welcome me home like the father in the story?"

"Every chance in the world," said Señor Anuncio. "Every chance in the world."

Then he told the young man how he had been at Nogales and how the old father had crept up to listen to the story and had told him how he longed for his son. "Could it be," asked Señor Anuncio, "that you are that very son?"

The young man got up and straightened his shoulders. He looked Señor Anuncio straight in the eye. "Yes, I am. And this very night I will leave here and start back to my father. I will find a job and work hard and prove that I am sorry for my foolishness."

"Good!" said Señor Anuncio. "What happiness there is going to be in the village of Nogales!"

# 74.
# *Roberto and the Rabbits*
## Around 1970

In the beautiful Andes Mountains about three miles from the village of Cachipay in Colombia, stood a tiny adobe house. This is where nine-year-old Roberto lived with his family.

Roberto's father had died, so Mother and the eight children were alone. The youngest child was only a few months old. How could they make a living without Father? Mother worked very hard on the little farm. Roberto and the brothers and sisters who were old enough worked very hard also. They all helped Mother raise bananas, oranges, and coffee. They helped load them on their little donkey to take them over the rocky mountain road to market.

But no matter how hard they worked, they never had quite enough money to buy the food they needed. Sometimes they were hungry when they went to bed.

One day baby brother became sick. Roberto saw the worried look on his mother's face as she tried to comfort the baby. The baby fretted. His little body was hot with fever.

"Mother," asked Roberto, "is our baby going to die?"

"Oh, no!" said Mother anxiously. "But we must take him to a doctor."

While the older children picked coffee, Roberto and his mother took the baby and hurried to Cachipay. Up and down the mountains they walked. Finally they came to the last long climb and then they were in the village.

The doctor examined baby brother. He gave him a shot and some medicine. Then he said to Mother, "Mrs. Rojas, the baby will be better soon. But you must give him more milk, and you and your children should eat more meat."

Roberto saw the hurt, tired look in his mother"s face. He knew that she wanted to give them more milk and meat—but how could she?

As they walked home again, Roberto noticed how his mother's shoulders drooped. Her face was sad. "She is tired," he thought. "Baby brother is heavy."

Roberto also kept thinking about their problem. How could they get more to eat? Suddenly something popped into his mind. He knew a man named Don Gene at the Colegio Americano, or American School, at Cachipay. Don Gene taught people to take care of rabbits and when they knew how, he gave them a pair. This was to help people get more meat to eat.

Why, that would be the very thing! Roberto was so excited about his new thought that he hopped, skipped, and jumped down the road.

That afternoon, he hurried to do all the jobs that were his. Then he asked his mother, "May I go to the Colegio?"

"Yes," said his mother. "You have helped me so much today. Go and have a good time."

Roberto fairly ran all the way to the Colegio. Don Gene was at the rabbit cages when Roberto arrived.

"Hello, Roberto!" he said. "What can I do for you?"

Roberto told him about his plan. "I would like to learn how to build a rabbit cage and how to care for rabbits," he said.

Done Gene was glad Roberto had come. They built a rabbit cage together. Then they fed the rabbits so Roberto could learn how it was done.

"Roberto," said Don Gene, "I have just the right pair of rabbits for you. But you must take very good care of them. They will soon have babies. When the baby rabbits are big enough, you must give two away. It has to be a boy rabbit and a girl rabbit and you must give them to someone else who needs meat to eat."

Roberto promised.

That evening Don Gene and Roberto carried the rabbit cage with the pair of rabbits in it up and down the mountain paths to Roberto's house.

Roberto took very good care of the rabbits. In a few weeks, early one morning, Roberto had a surprise. When he looked into the cage, he saw five tiny baby rabbits cuddled together in a little nest.

"Mother! Mother!" he shouted. "Come and see my baby rabbits!"

The baby rabbits grew fast and when they were big enough, Roberto did just as Don Gene had asked him to do. Roberto gave two bunnies—a pair—to another family.

Soon there were more and more bunnies. Mother fixed the most delicious rabbit dinners. Mother, Roberto and his brothers and sisters had all the meat they needed, and so did another family because Roberto remembered to give a pair away.

**116**

# 75.
# *The Importance of Every Life*
## Around 1930

Susie Isaak was a good nurse. She worked in a hospital in the town of Filadelfia in Paraguay. She was always very busy. But now she was especially busy. A sickness called malaria had broken out in that area so more people than they could handle came to the hospital for treatment. The doctor and the nurses were all tired.

One evening when the doctor had already gone home, Sister Susie, as everybody called her, heard someone come into the hospital with very quick steps. It was Missionary Gerhard Giesbrecht.

"Sister Susie," he said all out of breath, "will you accept a sick Indian child? The Indians have burned and left their camp because someone there has died. That is their custom. This baby was left behind. Can you take it?"

"Yes, yes, of course," said Sister Susie. "Bring the child to me."

Missionary Giesbrecht hurriedly drove away in his wagon and soon came back with a bundle on his lap.

The nurses ran to the wagon. "Please unwrap the child quickly," said Mr. Giesbrecht. "I don't know whether it is still alive."

Sister Susie took the child in her arms and unwrapped it. It was still breathing, but it was just skin and bones. She had never seen a child as thin as this one. She carried it immediately to one of the rooms and laid it into a child's bed. It was a boy about a year old.

With an eye-dropper Sister Susie put some water into his mouth. He moved a little bit, but the other nurses said, "Sister Susie, you can't help- that child. He is dying."

Sister Susie knew the nurses should go home and have a rest. She herself stayed to take care of the Indian baby boy.

She boiled some milk and every few minutes dropped some of it into his tiny mouth. Toward morning the baby opened his eyes for the first time.

When the doctor came to make his rounds, Sister Susie told him about the Indian baby. He looked at it and then said. "Sister Susie, don't you have enough work to do without taking care of this child? It is hopeless. It can't live."

"Doctor," said Sister Susie. "Every life is important. We must help him live."

"The hospital is full," said the doctor curtly. "Take it out immediately. I will not allow it to stay here."

Sister Susie took the baby in her arms. She carried it out of the room, wondering where to put the little boy. Her steps took her to the laundry. She borrowed a clothes hamper and put the baby into it. Then she carried the hamper outside on the porch and set it on a chair. When evening came she carried it into the laundry.

That first night, when the doctor had gone home and the other patients were taken care of, Sister Susie walked slowly into the operating room. She opened a big window and knelt down beside it. The stars shone and sparkled in the velvety blue sky. She looked up and prayed, "You know, Lord, that I have taken this child because I think you want him to live. Help me. Show me what to do. They will need the clothes hamper in the laundry, and I have nowhere to lay the child."

Sister Susie arose from her knees, comforted. She knew her prayer was answered. The Creator of heaven and earth would provide for the child.

One day soon afterwards, two high school students came to the hospital bringing a baby basket. It had a nice mattress in it and beautiful netting from a bridal veil to keep the mosquitos away. The students said, "Our neighbor heard that you had an Indian baby in the hospital and she thought you might be able to use her baby basket."

Sister Susie thanked them. She had not talked to other people about her need. She knew it was an answer to her prayer.

The nurses placed the baby into the pretty basket. No baby there had ever had such a beautiful little bed.

Missionary Giesbrecht often came to see the baby. He begged the doctor to examine him and work out a prescription for his feeding. Finally the doctor consented. After that the baby grew stronger every day. Soon he sat up and began to play.

The time came when a couple by the name of Teichrieb took the little Indian boy into their home as their very own. They called him Hans.

Little Hans Teichrieb soon learned to speak. Later he attended the village school where he learned the German language like all the other little boys in the village. He learned the Bible stories. He learned to know and love God.

Sister Susie saw little Hans grow up to be a young man. She was happy when he did well in school and when, later on, he decided to follow Christ. Finally he became a teacher and a preacher among his own Indian people and also the mayor of their settlement.

The years went by and Sister Susie became an old, old lady, but she was always glad to see Hans Teichrieb. She still remembered the time when she had held him as a little baby in her arms. She thanked God for the miracle of his life.

# 76.
# *Who Cares?*
## About 1930

John draped his towel on the bar at the foot of his bunk bed, hung his toothbrush on the nail, and slipped under the covers. He could hardly wait until the other boys in the dormitory were quiet and he could just lie there and think.

Now what was it again that Uncle Frank, the housefather, had said before he had prayed with them? "God cares about each one of you! You can tell him what is troubling you." And then Uncle Frank had talked to God as if he could see God in the room.

John had never heard of such a thing before. Could he really tell God how he felt about his mother leaving him and Dad? If his mother didn't care about him, how could he know for sure that God did?

John decided he wouldn't tell God. He doubted whether God would care to hear his troubles. And anyway, how did he know that God could really hear what he was saying?

The next day John almost forgot about his hurt. There were so many interesting things to see in this boarding school called *Academia Los Pinares* where his father had brought him. There was Amos, the school donkey, and Tiki, the little monkey. John liked to give her a banana because then she would hug him. It felt strange to have her hairy arms around his neck, but it was fun. And the boys showed him the fort they were building behind the school. He would be able to help them.

But when he watched the big flock of parrots

fly overhead, he wished he could fly home with them. And in school when the teacher stopped talking, he thought of his mother again and wondered whether she ever thought of him. Did God care about that? Apparently Uncle Frank thought so.

One day John heard the children shouting, "Uncle Paul is coming! Uncle Paul is coming!"

"Who is Uncle Paul?" John managed to ask as they ran toward the car turning in at the gate.

"He is our dentist," gasped one of the boys running beside him.

John couldn't understand why anyone should be that anxious to see a dentist, but he kept on running since everyone else did.

He soon found out that Uncle Paul, the dentist, usually stayed for several days and that the children loved him so much because he told them stories after supper.. John had never heard such wonderful stories. There were stories about animals, stories about boys and girls, and stories about people long ago who knew God.

One day after Uncle Paul had told a story, he said, "God cares about all people. He cares about you."

There it was again! God cared about all people as Uncle Frank had said.

That night when Uncle Frank came to say good-night to the boys and to pray with them, he made a special stop at John's bed and ran his hand affectionately over John's hair. John suddenly thought, "Uncle Frank cares about me." It made him feel all warm and happy inside.

John did a lot of thinking that night in his bunk bed. Before he knew it, he found himself telling God all about his mother and father. He was telling God about himself and how homesick he was.

He knew God was listening. He knew now that God cared.

# 77.
# *We Were Strangers and They Took Us In*
## 1981

A group of about thirty students from the Mennonite seminary in Asuncion, Paraguay, together with their music directors, David and Alice Suderman, were on the way to the Friesland Colony to give a concert. They had just been in Volendam and now their bus was slipping and slithering along slowly on a very muddy road to their next destination.

It was drizzling. The driver was handling the bus very well, but halfway to Friesland, there was a barricade. The road was closed. All traffic had to stop because of the mud.

What now? Fortunately the driver was allowed to drive the bus into a little Paraguayan village called *Rosario*, but where would they get food? Where would they get lodging? They did not know a single person in this place. Would they just have to stay on the bus until it stopped raining? That could be several days and several nights. There certainly was no possibility now of making it to the Friesland church in time for their program.

The bus had stopped in front of a little restaurant, but it was too small for the whole bus full of people. Gerhard Penner, the man who was responsible to find food and lodging on the tour, decided to go out and see whether he could find any other place where they could buy something to eat. After an hour or two he came back to the bus full of hungry people and said he had found another little restaurant. If they split up between the two restaurants they would all get something to eat.

That solved the first problem. But where would they stay for the night? There were no hotels in this village. On the bus were four student couples with children. Two were tiny babies and two were a little over a year old. Dr. and Mrs. Suderman were an elderly couple. Would they have to sit in the bus all night?

Gerhard Penner called back to the Volendam Colony, where they had just been, to see whether the people there could help them. Yes, they would be most happy to house the whole group, they said, but because of the barricade they could only come to within seven kilometers of Rosario to get them. If anyone wanted to walk that far in the rain and the mud they would pick them up there.

Some of the people could not possibly walk. Gerhard Penner tried everywhere to rent a horse and buggy but there was none to be found. Finally fifteen students decided to walk in order to be picked up by the people from Volendam. The others decided to stay in the bus.

Gerhard Penner and the bus driver went out to see if they could find lodging for the others. They were gone a long time. Finally they came back.

Gerhard was jubilant. "I have great news!" he called. "We went to see the mayor of the village and he said they have a guest house here that a German businessman built for himself some time ago and gave to the village when he left. The mayor said we are very welcome to stay there."

"That's wonderful!" called the people in the bus. Immediately they all piled out and walked the three blocks to the guest house.

But they were just looking at the rooms when a Paraguayan came in and asked the Sudermans to follow him. They were not to stay in this house. What could this mean? The Sudermans walked down the street with the man. He took them straight to the mayor's house.

At the door stood the mayor, Mr. Caballero. He stretched out his hands and called warmly, "Welcome! Welcome! You will stay right here!"

He took them to an extra room they had and said, "Put down your suitcase and come and join us in the living room. We are having some guests."

Mrs. Caballero was not at home yet. She didn't know what had happened. By this time Mr. Caballero had invited the Gerhard Penners with their little boy to stay at the house too. What would Mrs. Caballero say when she saw all these guests that were to stay overnight?

When she came in and was told what had happened, she immediately said to Mrs. Suderman, "Come with me. I don't want you to stay in the extra room. You are to sleep in our bedroom. It is closer to the bathroom and it will be more comfortable for you."

She put clean linens on their bed and insisted that the Sudermans take their room.

The Sudermans were overwhelmed. They had never seen these people before and yet they were showing them this kind of hospitality!

The next morning Mrs. Caballero fixed breakfast for all of them, and then the Sudermans and the Penners walked back to join the others at the guest house.

But that was by no means the end of their happy experience in the village of Rosario. Around noon they suddenly noticed people bringing a big grill and charcoal and lots of meat. It happened to be a holiday and so the people of the village decided to have the celebration near the guest house so their visitors could join them.

Everybody had a great time. After they had eaten, people visited with each other. The people of Rosario knew that this was a choir group and so they asked them to sing. Only half the choir was there, but never had they sung with such warmth and gratitude!

"This evening you must come to the parish and sing for my people there," said a priest in the group.

So that evening the choir group went over to the priest's home. The people gathered quickly.

Those that had no room, stood around outside. Across the street the people flung open their doors so they could hear better.

After the singing, the people immediately treated the guests to bottled drinks. Then the priest said to Dr. Suderman, "Now, when can you come and teach our people to sing? We love to sing. We want to have a song festival Couldn't you come and help us?"

Since it was still raining, the choir group stayed in Rosario another night. Finally on the next day it cleared up. The group that had gone back to Volendam joined them and they were able to leave. They said good-bye to their new friends. What a good time they had had! It was hard to believe that only two nights ago when they arrived in that village they had known no one.

As they started on their way, a student said softly, "We were strangers and they took us in."

# The Good News
# in North America

# 78.
# *A Story of the Cheyenne*

Many years ago, the Cheyenne people, or Sisistas as they called themselves, moved from one part of the northern continent to another. One day a small group of Sisistas went out ahead of the major body of the tribe. They knew that perhaps they were infringing on the hunting grounds or the territory of other peoples, so they were very careful.

Suddenly they came upon some people who had been watching them. They stopped short. They thought surely they would be attacked. They had infringed on the hunting grounds or territory of these people and so they could expect to be driven out. The two groups stood apart from each other.

Finally one of the Sisistas said something to the men who were with him. The other groups also started talking to each other. They were each talking among themselves. Somehow they began to listen to each other. To their surprise they found out that both groups were speaking the same language! The Sisistas and the *Sotai,* as the second group was called, although they were complete strangers to each other, were two groups of Cheyenne.

At first they feared each other. Both groups thought the other might start to fight. But since they spoke the same language they began to communicate with each other. There were two distinct cultures but they each accepted a portion of what the other group had to offer. Finally the two cultures merged. The best of both the Sisistas and the Sotai gave rise to a long-standing friendship between these two peoples. For decades and centuries they have now walked down the road of life together.

Many years ago a missionary from Kansas, J.B. Ediger, came to what is now known as the *Clinton Indian Community.* He came into a culture completely different from the one he and his family were used to. How would the people respond to this white man? It was a very turbulent time. The government had just broken up their reservation. The Cheyenne had suffered much at the hands of the white people.

But the Sisistas remembered their story. They remembered when they had met the Sotai, a group of people who were strangers, but who became friends when they began listening to each other.

So the Cheyenne welcomed the missionary. Names are extremely important and highly significant in their culture so they decided to give him a name. What kind of a name should they give this man? They decided to give him the name *Sotai,* just as the people were called who had become their friends so long ago and who were now one with them.

"Sotai" lived among them. He learned their language. He loved the Cheyenne so well that he brought them the good news of Jesus Christ in word and deed for well over forty years. He became one of them, just like the Sotai tribe had so long ago.

# 79.
# *Why Had He Failed?*
## Around 1880

Samuel S. Haury went out to the Arapaho Indian territory in Oklahoma as a missionary in the year 1880. He wanted to tell the Indian people that God loves all the people in the world alike and wants them to love him.

One Sunday morning Samuel Haury and another missionary, D. B. Hirschler, were teaching Sunday school. All was peaceful in the little room as Samuel Haury told the Indian children about Jesus. But suddenly Samuel Haury paused and listened.

He thought he heard the pounding of horses' hoofs and yelling in the distance. The whole class looked startled.

Samuel Haury strode to the window just in time to see three men come galloping through the gate. A group of Indians on horseback were close behind them.

"Save us, save us," yelled one of the white men.

Samuel Haury rushed out, leaving the class with Mr. Hirschler. By this time the men had jumped off their horses, run into one of the little houses on the yard, and slammed the door shut.

The Indians thundered into the yard and pulled up their horses in front of Samuel Haury.

"Those men killed Running Buffalo," Left Hand Bull, their leader, said slowly and distinctly.

Samuel Haury was stunned. Running Buffalo was his friend. He had just had dinner with him the day before. It was clear that the Indians were going to kill the white men for what they had done. It was also clear that the white men had come to him for protection. What should he do?

Missionary Haury knew that he must try to bring about understanding between these two groups. He must try to prevent further bloodshed.

"What happened?" he asked the Indians.

"These three cowboys were driving several hundred ponies north," said Left Hand Bull. "They wanted to drive them across Running Buffalo's land. When they got there, Running Buffalo asked them to give him two horses as payment for allowing them to do this, but the cowboys refused to pay. Instead they shot Running Buffalo. Now we will kill the cowboys."

The Indians were ready to storm the building where the cowboys were hiding, but Missionary Haury stopped them. "We must find a way to solve this problem. Let me talk to the cowboys."

The three cowboys were shaking with fear when Samuel Haury came to them.

"Tell me what happened," said the missionary.

"We were driving 400 ponies north to Kansas," said E. M. Horton, the leader. "The usual crossing at the North Canadian River was flooded, so we had to take the route across Running Buffalo's land. He demanded two horses in payment. That is stupid. We told him so, and suddenly he shot. So we shot back and killed him."

"Running Buffalo's dog soldier friends were after us immediately," gasped one of the other cowboys. "All our ponies scattered across the prairie. We just barely got away."

"The Indians want revenge. They will kill you unless we find a way of reconciliation," said Missionary Haury. "I will try to persuade them to disarm and talk with you."

"No way," said E. M. Horton. "We knew there was a telegraph office in this little build ing here at the time when this was a military post. We have already wired the United States soldiers at Fort Reno to come and help us. They are on their way. We will be alright if you will just hold off the Indians for a little while until they get here."

"No, no," said Missionary Haury. "We must come to some understanding."

He hurried out, closing the door behind him.

"My friends," said Samuel Haury to the Indians. "You know that Running Buffalo was my friend. I am very sad that he is dead. But I do not want any more people killed and another war to start. Will two of your leaders put away their guns and come with me to the middle of the yard to talk with the cowboys? I will try to have them put away their guns and also come out here."

The Indians were silent for a while. Then the two leaders put down their guns and walked with Missionary Haury to a spot near the telegraph office where the cowboys had locked themselves in.

"Mr. Horton," called Samuel Haury. "Put down your gun and come out to discuss the problem."

"No, I will not put down my gun, and I will not come out," shouted E. M. Horton. "The Indians have made us lose 400 ponies, and we will not negotiate. The U.S. soldiers will talk to them with their guns."

Missionary Haury turned to the Indians. "Would you be willing to round up the ponies and put them in the corral here, until we can settle the whole matter?"

The Indians respected Missionary Haury. They knew he was their friend. After a long discussion some of them rode away and in time brought all the ponies into the corral.

In the meantime, during that long Sunday afternoon, the Indians pointed their guns at the telegraph office and the cowboys held their guns ready inside.

Samuel Haury walked back and forth. It was agony. Would he be able to prevent another war between the Indians and the whites? Would the U.S. soldiers arrive before the Indians had killed the three men in the telegraph office? And what would the soldiers do to the Indians?

Finally the U. S. cavalry came.

"What's the problem?" asked the captain.

Missionary Haury explained what had happened.

Each side insisted that the other side had fired first. One thing was certain, however. The three cowboys had killed Running Buffalo and so the murderers were taken into custody to be tried in court.

The captain bargained with the Indians regarding a fair settlement. Finally Left Hand Bull, their leader, accepted one half of Horton's horses to settle the matter.

Missionary Haury was relieved. It looked as if everyone was going to be treated fairly. But there was more to come.

E. M. Horton was tried in a civil court in Wichita, Kansas. The jury said he was not guilty even though there was no question that he had killed Running Buffalo. Not only that. The government gave an order that the horses that had been given to the Indians as settlement had to be returned to Horton.

Missionary Haury, who had testified at the trial, went back to the mission station with a heavy heart. He had not been able to bring about reconciliation between the Indians and the white men. justice had not been done. The Indians were still angry, and the white men did not repent. He had wanted to bring the Indians the good news of God's love that was for everyone alike. Why had he failed?

# 80.
# In Their Own Language
*(Rodolphe Petter)*
1865-1947

Over a hundred years ago in Switzerland there lived a little boy called Rodolphe Petter. One night when he was ten years old, he was awakened by the village bell. In the quietness that followed, he felt very clearly that God was calling him. He answered, telling God that he wanted to do whatever God wanted him to do.

Some time later, Rodolphe's brother Auguste had a dream. In the morning he came to Rodolphe and said, "Rodolphe, I dreamed about you. I saw you standing before a large group of Indians preaching to them in their own language." Rodolphe always remembered this dream. It was very important to him. He believed that it was God's way of telling him what he should do.

So Rodolphe prepared himself to be a missionary. He first of all had to learn German in order to study at the missions institute. He had grown up with the French language. Then he studied Hebrew , Greek, Latin, theology, and medicine. Finally he and his young wife, Marie, went to North America. There they had to learn English.

In 1891 Rodolphe and Marie were ordained as missionaries in Halstead, Kansas, and went to Oklahoma to start their work. Their first task was to learn the language of the Cheyenne. That was more difficult than any of the other languages they had learned because it was not written down. A number of the Cheyenne people at the mission station in Cantonment helped them. In order to learn more quickly, the Petters lived in tents among the people so they could talk with each other. As they mastered the language, they translated parts of the Bible and also prepared a Cheyenne Grammar and an English-Cheyenne dictionary. They could hardly wait until they could take the good news of Jesus Christ to the Cheyenne people living in Oklahoma.

At last they thought they could try it. In a wagon drawn by a pair of mules, they set out across the endless prairie to visit the Cheyenne settlements along Deer Creek, and the Washita and Canadian rivers. It was hot and water was hard to find.

The Petters were concerned when they neared the Washita camp. They had heard that the Indians living there did not want to be friends with the white people. But they drove straight to the tepee of Chief Red Moon.

Chief Red Moon came out. He walked steadily toward them and stood still.

Mr. Petter spoke slowly in the Cheyenne language. He asked, "Are you Chief Red Moon? We would like to pitch our tent here in your camp."

"Who are you?" asked Chief Red Moon. "How is it that you, a white man, speak Cheyenne?"

But before Mr. Petter could answer, Chief Red Moon smiled. He said, "I know you are a friend. Our people in Cantonment have told me. Dwell in peace in our camp."

How relieved the Petters were! They put up their tent. The Indians brought them food to eat and water to drink. The Petters sat outside to eat their supper. Soon the children in the camp crept closer. They wanted to see these strange white people. They pointed at the hair on Mr. Petter's upper lip and whispered.

But then Chief Red Moon came by and saw what was happening. "Don't bother these people, children," he said sternly. "A good Cheyenne does not gaze on those who eat."

The next morning Chief Red Moon and some

of the leading men came to the Petter's tent. They all sat down and smoked the peace pipe. Then the chief asked, "Why have you come to us?"

"We have come across the big water to tell you about God in your own language," said Mr. Petter.

"Good," said Chief Red Moon. "We will listen to what you have to say about God. We will meet tonight in the woods nearby and you may speak."

That evening the Petters went to the place the chief had indicated. Around a huge fire under the tall trees sat Chief Red Moon and his men. They were smoking the peace pipe and passing it from one to another. Above them the sky was filled with stars.

Chief Red Moon introduced Mr. Petter. Then Mr. Petter read to them some of the passages of the Bible he had translated into Cheyenne. They all listened carefully. It was the first time they had heard God's Word in their own language.

Mr. Petter told them that the message he had was that God loves all people, regardless of their race. They all bowed their heads during the closing prayer.

Chief Red Moon thanked Mr. Petter. He asked him to come again and explain the message he had brought. Then the peace pipe was smoked again. Each man took a few puffs and passed it on. Through the shadows came the women carrying food. They served everyone venison and Indian fry bread. Then they all parted in peace.

For many years Rodolphe and Marie Petter came to bring the Indians more words from the Bible they had translated. Each year they could speak the language a little better so they could explain what the message meant.

That was the beginning of Rodolphe Petter's fifty-six years of work among the Southern and Northern Cheyenne in Oklahoma and Montana. He stood among them many times as his brother Auguste had seen him in his dream. And he spoke to the Cheyenne in their own language.

# 81.
# *A Pulpit, an Organ, and a Stove*

Huge clouds were gathering over the little Cheyenne settlement in Busby, Montana. The thunder rolled ominously across the sky and the lightning showed with ever increasing frequency the little houses clustered around a church. The people had sought shelter and were anxiously watching whether the funnel of a tornado would appear in the clouds.

Suddenly it came. The tornado swept through Busby in half a minute and left only wreckage behind. No people were killed but as they came out of their shelters they saw that the church was gone.

They all came and silently stood at the spot where there had been a building. Then one man said, "The church has been destroyed. The Great Spirit is angry because our Cheyenne religion was not taught there."

Many of the Cheyenne people nodded their heads. There was a murmur of approval in the crowd.

But then a woman slowly walked to the spot where the church had stood and where she had received so many blessings from God, the great heavenly Father.

She pointed to the pulpit, which the tornado, in its mysterious way, had left standing exactly where it had always stood.

"Look," she said. "The pulpit has remained. It is because the true word of God was spoken there."

She walked over to the organ, which had also been spared. "And this organ helped us sing praises to God," she said. "It has been left to us so we can continue to use it to the glory of our heavenly Father."

Then she looked over to the stove, standing alone in the wreckage of the kitchen. "From the stove came fire," she continued. "It is the symbol of the Holy Spirit. We must continue to build the Church of Jesus Christ in this spot. God has clearly shown us that his blessing is upon us."

The people were quiet. There was much to think about. The church in Busby was built again.

# 82.
# A Peace Chief
## (Lawrence Hart)

Once there was a little Cheyenne boy called Black Beaver. His English name was Lawrence Hart. But his grandfather called him Black Beaver.

Black Beaver loved his grandfather in whose home he grew up. The old man was a Cheyenne chief and told Black Beaver many stories about his people. They had been brave. The dog soldiers had fought with great courage. But the bravest of all, said his grandfather, were the chiefs who believed in peace. Black Beaver loved to hear his grandfather talk about the peace chiefs, but he was sorry that there were no dog soldiers anymore. He wished he could have become one.

One day Black Beaver was picking cotton. It was hot. Finally he lay down on his cotton sack to rest for a while and to look up into the blue sky. Suddenly he heard a roaring noise. In perfect formation a group of aircraft swept over him and disappeared into the distance!

In that instant Black Beaver knew what he wanted to do. He would become Lawrence Hart, the great pilot, and fight like the brave Cheyenne dog soldiers had done in the past.

So that is what the young Lawrence worked at—to become a pilot. He knew he needed to go to college to get the necessary preparation. Arthur Friesen, the pastor of his home church in Clinton, Oklahoma, encouraged him to go to Bethel College.

Lawrence soon found out that at Bethel College a great deal of emphasis was put on serving others and on peacemaking. There were many people who showed by the way they lived their Christian lives, that this was very important to them. But Lawrence did not pay too much attention to it. After all, wasn't he going to go into the military and become a great pilot?

During the second year at Bethel, Lawrence met a student named Larry Kaufman. They were in the same class and lived in the same dormitory. They became close friends.

Larry shared with Lawrence his dreams of going into mission work. He was opposed to war and violence. He wanted to become a peacemaker. Lawrence shared with Larry his dreams of becoming a pilot in the air force. He wanted to become a great flier. He wanted the members of his tribe to be proud of him. The two dreams were the opposite of each other. But that did not matter. Larry and Lawrence were friends. They listened to each other. They respected each other.

After two years the two young men went in opposite directions. Larry went to Africa under the Congo Inland Mission. Lawrence went on to study to be a pilot.

Lawrence worked hard. He was determined. He studied math and physics. He studied hydraulics. He studied all of the technical systems that go into an aircraft. Finally he reached his goal. He became a pilot, a marine pilot, a jet fighter pilot, and finally a special weapons pilot, tutored by the best fliers of the Korean War.

The pilots who were teaching the students how to deliver the special weapons of destruction, showed them a film. The film showed how they had shot down the planes and the pilots. The scenes were horrible. Many of the student pilots were shocked when they saw what it is like to kill people.

Lawrence knew then that as a pilot in the war he would be shooting women and children and other innocent people, just like his own Cheyenne people had been brutally shot down by soldiers in various stages of American history. It made him think. Was this really what he wanted to do? In the midst of his struggle, he heard sad news. His friend, Larry Kaufman, had died while he was doing his peaceful mission work in Africa in the name of Christ.

All the memories of Larry rushed into his mind, all that his friend had stood for, all the good things he had hoped to do. Lawrence knew that the love of Christ that had motivated Larry was something he wanted. The great models of the peace chiefs his grandfather had told him about rose large in his memory. Lawrence Hart received a new vision.

He got out of the air force as soon as possible. He studied to be a Christian minister and became the pastor of his home church. His tribe respected him highly and made him a Cheyenne chief. By his life Lawrence showed that many of the traditions of his people and their view of life agreed with what Christ had taught. He was a traditional Cheyenne and yet a committed Christian.

The little boy, Black Beaver, had become Lawrence Hart, the peace chief. At the ceremony in which he became a chief of the tribe, his mother gave him the name Chief-in-the-Sky.

## 83.
# *He Received a Call*
## *(Elijah McKay)*
## Around 1960

Elijah McKay was a young Indian in Manitoba. He came to know the Lord Jesus Christ and committed his whole heart and life to him when he was about twenty-two years old. From that point on his greatest desire was to tell others what he had discovered. He could not keep it to himself. Everything had become new. He wanted to share this good news with others so that they too might come to know the Savior.

Elijah immediately started preparing himself for the task of working for God. He went to Bible school for three years. After his graduation he was assigned to go to an Indian reservation to tell the good news there. Elijah could hardly wait. He was all ready to go.

But then Elijah started getting nosebleeds. He

**130**

had bad headaches. When he went to a doctor, it was discovered that he had tuberculosis. Instead of going to the reservation, Elijah had to go to a sanitarium for treatment.

Elijah was crushed. He prayed to God over and over again, "Get me out of here in some miraculous way so I can go to the reservation and do your will there."

But God did not do what Elijah asked. He performed no miracle for him. For eighteen months Elijah had to stay in the hospital. When he was well enough to come out, he went to school in Brandon to get a better education.

Since he had not been allowed to go to the reservation where he had wanted to go in the first place, Elijah forgot about the call to the Christian ministry. He still believed in Christ; he still went to church. But he decided he had better make some money and make a future for himself.

Elijah McKay did very well. He got a good job. He married and had children. He became rich.

Everything was going well when one day he got a nosebleed again. He had headaches. He again had a spot on his lungs. His tuberculosis was back again. Once more he had to go to the hospital. His carefree life was over.

Now Elijah had much time to think about his past life and about what it all meant. He realized now that he had developed his own plan of how he was going to work for God. He had not relied on the Holy Spirit. Instead of allowing God to tell him, he had been trying to tell God what to do.

This time he prayed, "God, please show me the way. If you want me to serve you in a special way, then tell me yourself. If you show me where you want me to go, I shall be glad to go. Otherwise I will go back to my job when I get better."

That night Elijah had a dream. He saw himself sitting as director at the desk of the Mennonite Native Social Centre called *Your Opportunities Unlimited (YOU)* in Winnipeg!

Native people take dreams very seriously. just as God spoke to men, women, and children in biblical times, Indians believe strongly that he still does. But Elijah laughed when he awoke. How could he become director of YOU? He had heard about the center and he knew he was not qualified to do the things that were being done there.

"You will have to do better than that, God, if you want to deal with me," prayed Elijah McKay.

The second night he had exactly the same dream. He was a director of the Mennonite Native Social Centre.

Again Elijah said, "No way, Lord. You've got to get me out of this hospital. I will be glad to do your will and go where you want me to go, but only if I really know what your will is."

On the third night he had the same dream.

The next morning his wife came to see him. He said to her, "I got a job last night. I got a job. I know what I am going to do when I leave the hospital."

Elijah explained to her what he meant. He told her how God had spoken to him in a dream and told him what to do.

At first his wife could hardly believe that Elijah was serious, but he said to her, "Send my resignation to the company where I worked. I will not be going back there when I am well."

After that things began to happen. A few days after his dream, Jake Unrau of the native Mennonite center came to see him. A friend of Elijah's who worked at the center dropped in. Elijah could ask him anything he wanted to about the center.

Just as soon as he was out of the hospital, Elijah went to the center to see about the job God had shown him in his dream. Elijah meant business. And about six months later he was sitting behind the desk as a director of Your Opportunities Unlimited (YOU), just as he had seen himself in his dream.

# 84.

# *A Surprise*

## *(Elijah McKay)*
## Around 1950

A young Indian called Elijah McKay was hospitalized in a tuberculosis sanitarium in Manitoba. He was a Christian and wanted more than anything else to go to the Indian reservations to tell the people there the good news of salvation in Christ. But he could not leave the hospital. He could not understand why God would allow such a thing to happen to him when he was so eager to serve him.

There were many native people in the sanitarium. Elijah had a lot of time on his hands, so he went to see the other patients. He talked with them. He told them about Christ and what he had done for him, and organized a Bible study group. More and more Indians came to it.

One of those Indians was a man by the name of Paul. Paul was especially eager to study the Bible, and in time, through Elijah's ministry, accepted the Lord Jesus Christ as his Savior. He was exuberant in his newfound faith. He wanted to tell others about Christ. At that time doctors did not as yet have the necessary medications to heal tuberculosis and Paul could expect to be in the sanitarium for years. But he was healed in six months and went home.

Elijah, however, had to stay on in the sanitarium much longer. Finally, he too got out of the hospital and gradually started working again, but he never heard from his friend Paul.

After about ten years, Elijah was doing Voluntary Service in Ontario for the Mennonite Central Committee under the Indian Affairs Department. In the course of his work he was sent to many different Indian reservations.

Usually when he got to a reservation, he would ask himself, "Whom do I know here?" One day as he was thinking this, something reminded him of Paul. Even though he had not had any contact with him during all these years, he had heard he was supposed to be in this area.

"Do you know Paul Kekika?" he asked some people.

"Yes, we do," they said. "He lives over there across the lake."

Elijah immediately phoned Paul. Paul was very glad to hear his voice and invited him to come over to see him.

In the evening when Elijah came to the place where Paul lived, he had a great big surprise. There in the wilderness stood a little church and it was packed with men, women, and children, gathered for a worship service. How could this be?

Paul said, "Elijah, I got to know Christ through you when you were in the hospital. This is the result. My brother and I are pastoring this group of people and we built our own church. All this came about because you helped me."

Elijah bowed his head in wonder at the majesty of God. He had not understood it then. But he recognized now, ten years later, how marvelously God had used his illness to bring the good news to a group of people who had never heard it before.

# 85.
# *The Labrador Doctor*
## *(Wilfred Grenfell)*
## 1865-1940

Wilfred Grenfell is often referred to as *the Labrador doctor*. Many years ago he came out from England as a young missionary and sailed his hospital ship up the Labrador coast every summer and traveled by dog sled in winter. There was great hardship among people everywhere. When Dr. Grenfell came, he brought hope. People from long distances brought their sick to him.

First he gave medical help to those who needed it. Then he taught the people crowding around to sing gospel hymns and told them the story of Jesus. He always had food and clothing with him and distributed them to the very poor. All along the coast Dr. Grenfell was known and loved.

One summer he went farther north than he had ever been on his hospital ship. He reached Nachvak Inlet and steamed through the narrow entrance between steep rocks. Deeper and deeper into the inlet he went until he came to an Eskimo village. The manager of the Hudson Bay Company post, George Ford, came out to meet him. He had already heard of the famous Dr. Grenfell, but he also had an important message for the doctor.

"Several days ago a band of Eskimos came through here," he told him. "They carried a little boy with them who was very sick. I have since heard that he is dying in a tent some miles up the inlet."

Dr. Grenfell immediately set out to find the boy. He and his helpers climbed over great cliffs and slid down huge rocks. They looked and looked, but how would they ever find a tiny tent that was no bigger than one of the stones that lay around by the thousands on these mountains?

After two days, standing on a high peak on the mountain and using binoculars, they saw it! The tent was nestled among the rocks near a mighty waterfall. Quickly they climbed down to it. When they peeked into the tent they saw a boy, about eleven years old, lying under an old reindeer skin, staring at them with large eyes. They could see he was in great pain. The boy's name was Pomiuk.

Quickly Dr. Grenfell examined him. He saw Pomiuk had open sores because of a bad hip infection which had spread and made him very weak. His father had been murdered and his mother had left him. Another Eskimo couple was trying to take care of him.

Carefully and tenderly Dr. Grenfell and his helpers carried Pomiuk to the ship to take him to a hospital. On board the ship the doctor washed Pomiuk and treated his wounds. He gave him raw walrus meat which he knew Eskimos loved. Pomiuk lost his fears and watched the good doctor carefully. Soon he began to smile and talk. It didn't take long to learn the hymns Dr. Grenfell taught him. He lay on his deerskin on deck and sang happily. By the time the ship reached the hospital everybody on board loved Pomiuk.

There was a mystery about Pomiuk, however. When Dr. Grenfell had taken the filthy clothes off of Pomiuk in order to bathe him, he found a deerskin bag hanging around his neck. When he opened it, he found a letter from a Reverend Charles Carpenter in Boston and also his photograph.

"Do you know this man?" asked Dr. Grenfell, pointing to the photograph.

"Yes, me know him—me even love him," said Pomiuk in the few English words he knew.

The minister in Boston had met Pomiuk when the little Eskimo boy had been at the World's Fair in Chicago as part of an Eskimo group brought in as an attraction. When Mr. Carpenter found out that after the fair was over the Eskimo group had been left to find their way 2, 000 miles to their northern home, he became very much concerned about his little friend. He had tried for several years to locate Pomiuk.

When Pomiuk was safely in the hospital, Dr. Grenfell wrote to Charles Carpenter and told him what had happened. "He is still quite sick," he wrote. "We shall keep him in the hospital until next year. Perhaps then, God willing, I shall be able to take him to his northern country again. Would you pray for him?"

That Charles Carpenter certainly did, but he did something else. As a minister he was responsible for a children's page in a religious paper called the *Congregationalist*. He wrote Pomiuk's story in his "Corner" for the children. Then he added, "Let us remember this poor boy on the bleak Arctic shore. He belongs to us; let us take care of him."

The children who read the paper responded at once. They sent in enough money to pay for Pomiuk's stay at the hospital. Pomiuk had many friends now. They did not want him ever to be cold or lonely again.

Dr. Grenfell had to go to England for the winter. When he came back to Labrador he went to see Pomiuk as soon as he could.

Pomiuk greeted him with a big smile. "I am Gabriel Pomiuk now," he said. Moravian missionaries were also working in that area. They had taught Pomiuk many stories about Jesus and so Pomiuk wanted to be baptized to show that he was a Christian. At his baptism he was given the new name of *Gabriel*, the "Angel of Comfort" because with his bright smile and happy ways Pomiuk was a comfort to all in the hospital.

In the fall Dr. Grenfell suddenly got a message from the nurse at the hospital that Pomiuk was much worse. Even though it was very late in the year and the ice might close in on the ship, Dr. Grenfell steamed 2,000 miles to Indian Harbour where Pomiuk was in the hospital. He treated him as best he could, but soon after that the little Eskimo boy died.

Dr. Grenfell and all the nurses were very sad. The hospital seemed desolate without Pomiuk's laugh. But when they stepped outside the sky was aflame with the dancing northern lights. It seemed to them a sign of the joy there was in heaven as Gabriel Pomiuk, the Angel of Comfort, entered his heavenly home.

Dr. Grenfell never forgot Pomiuk. When, as an old man, the doctor wrote his book *Forty Years for Labrador*, he told about Pomiuk and the boys and girls all over the United States and Canada who had been his friends.

# 86.
# *Hospitality*
## (*Wilfred Grenfell*)
## 1865-1940

*Wilfred Grenfell, the Labrador doctor and missionary, helped all people regardless of what religion they belonged to. He believed that was Christ's way. He liked to tell the following story about how he himself was helped:*

One bitterly cold day in Labrador, the doctor was on his way to a patient who lived in a village many miles away. The doctor was traveling with his dog team, but since the distance was so great, he did not make it in one day. He stopped at the hut of a fisherman and asked if he could stay for the night.

The fisherman and his wife welcomed him with open arms. They served him hot cocoa made with milk and sugar. They gave him their bed and did everything to make him comfortable.

When Dr. Grenfell got up the next morning, he found, to his surprise, that his host was already gone. Since the doctor was not sure of the way to the village fourteen miles away where the patient lived, and because the snow was very deep, the fisherman had gone early to break and mark the trail to the doctor's next destination. He had also taken some milk and sugar to the host where Dr. Grenfell would stay in the next village. He knew the people there were so poor that they had no milk and sugar for cocoa and he did not want them to be embarrassed. He and his wife had a little bit that they saved for company.

Dr. Grenfell always closed this story by saying, "The man who walked to the village fourteen miles away to break the trail for me, was a Roman Catholic, the neighbor to whom he carried the milk and sugar, was a Methodist, and I am an English Episcopalian."

# 87.
# The Debt Is Paid
## (David Toews)
## 1870-1947

When David Toews was ten years old, he had more adventures than most boys can even dream about. He and his family left their comfortable home in Russia to migrate with a big group of families to Turkestan in Central Asia.

It was a long, long trip and very difficult. Slowly the long train of wagons made their way through high mountains, through cities, and finally through the endless deserts of Turkestan. Often David and his friends ran barefoot beside the wagons. When the train stopped, they lay down under the wagons to protect themselves from the burning sun.

But it wasn't all fun. Sometimes they ran out of food. Sometimes they could find no water. Sometimes they ran into terrible storms. More and more often people got sick. Many people died. One day, David, too, had a high fever when he became ill with smallpox.

Some of the things that David experienced were so terrible that he never wanted to talk about them. He never forgot them, however, and later they helped him understand other people when they were in trouble.

David's family did not stay in Turkestan. They decided to come to the United States.

Finally, when David was a young man, he became a teacher and went to Canada. Here much work awaited him. He was ordained as a minister and became a strong leader in the Mennonite church. Everything was preparing him for the special job he was to do someday.

World War I was raging in Europe. Finally there was a revolution in Russia. The Mennonites who had stayed there were in great trouble. Many were starving. Many had been killed. Many had lost their homes. Where should they go?

David remembered what it was like to be hungry and thirsty and sick and to have no home. "We must help our Mennonite people come to Canada," he said.

"That is impossible," said some of the other leaders. "These people in Russia have no money to pay for the trip. It will cost thousands and thousands of dollars. We can't collect that much money in our churches. It just won't work."

But David Toews was determined. Those people needed to get out of Russia. The right thing was to help them.

The Canadian Pacific Railway Company was willing to loan half a million dollars to bring the new immigrants to Canada. David Toews had confidence in his people in Russia and his people in North America that together they would be able to repay the debt.

The other leaders did not think so. They thought it was too big a risk. But David Toews personally signed the contract. He gave his word of honor that the debt would be paid.

The Mennonites in Russia had been anxiously waiting. Finally the day came when the first group could leave and come to Canada. Then another group came and another and another, until eventually 20,000 were able to settle in Canada. Much more money had to be borrowed from the railroad company. It became a two million dollar debt.

How happy the people were that they could once again live in peace, that they could worship God, and that they could bring up their children in the Christian faith!

They all started working hard in the new country.

The first thing many of them did was to save penny by penny, dollar by dollar, to pay off their travel debt. They would not buy anything for themselves until they could send in the money they owed. They knew David Toews had signed the loan contract because he trusted them.

Many others of the new immigrants wanted to pay their debts also, but they thought they would first buy some furniture, or some implements, or other things they needed. The debt could wait. David Toews had more and more headaches. The money was not coming in as it should, yet he had to make the promised payments to the railroad company.

Then there were some new immigrants who had no intention of paying their travel debt. They had soon forgotten how they and their children had suffered. They were now making money and they were going to keep it. They said, "That railroad company has enough money." It made David Toews sad. He had counted on his people to be honest.

Many years went by. David Toews had become an old man. He and other leaders in the church were still trying to collect the rest of the money. It was becoming more and more difficult because there was a depression and there were crop failures. Many of the immigrants had no money. Some had already died. Some were sick and could not pay. Was the debt never going to be paid? David Toews was weary.

But the church is a body of believers. They work together and help each other. When one part of the body hurts, the whole body hurts. The whole Mennonite church hurt because of the debt. So altogether, both in the United States and Canada, people pooled their resources and in November 1946 the whole amount was finally paid.

Jubilantly one of the church leaders went to David Toews. "The debt is paid," he told him. David Toews had become a very old man. He could not hear very well anymore. He did not understand.

"The debt is paid!" said his friend more loudly.

David Toews shook his head. He could not believe it.

But when he finally realized that it was indeed true, he bowed his head and wept. They were tears of joy and thanksgiving. His burden was gone. Several months later he died.

## 88.
# *How Can We Help?*
## Around 1940

A little church in Canada had a problem. A member of the congregation, Mr. Dyck, had just died. His widow had a very bad heart. Where should she go?

The Dycks had recently come from Europe. They had managed to buy a tiny little house, but it was so far away from the place where other members of the congregation lived that they would not be able to help Mrs. Dyck if she suddenly needed help. And she had no money to buy another lot.

The pastor and members of the congregation sat down together to see what they could do.

"Mrs. Dyck cannot stay where she is," said one member.

"No," they all agreed, "she cannot stay by herself."

"She has no children or relatives who could take her in. We simply must find a way to help her," said another.

They all nodded their heads. They wanted to help, but how? All the people in the congregation were pioneers in that area. They were all struggling just to make a bare living. No one had money. No one had a big enough house to take in another person.

Finally they all bowed their heads and prayed. "Show us, Father, how we can help. Give us the right—thoughts, that we might find a way."

Then they all sat and thought.

Finally somebody said, "You know, she could possibly stay in her little house if the house were not so far away from us."

"Perhaps we could move it," somebody else thought out loud.

"But where can we move it to?" asked another. "Lots are far too expensive and the lot where it is now standing has not been paid for."

They were all quiet.

Suddenly someone said, "The only lot we own together is the one on which our church stands. Why not move the little house to the corner of the church lot?"

Everybody sat up straight. "Yes, why not?" "The house is so tiny, it would have room there. She could even walk to church if she lived there."

"I could look in on her every day," volunteered one woman who lived across the street from the church, "and do her errands for her."

"If we attached a special light to her door, we would see it from our house if she turned it on to ask for help," said the pastor.

The problem was solved. Mrs. Dyck was delighted when she heard of the plan. The men in the congregation moved the little house to the churchyard. The women helped Mrs. Dyck fix it up inside and move everything into place. A string was attached near her bed so she could turn on the special light if she needed help.

Mrs. Dyck lived happily on the churchyard for many years right in the midst of the congregation. They loved her. They cared for her. She welcomed everyone that came to see her and in her wisdom contributed much to the life of the congregation. When she died that little spot on the churchyard seemed very empty.

## 89.
# *Her Gift*
## Around 1980

Katie Peters had always been a little shy. When other children talked loudly and confidently, she could not think of a word to say. When children laughed boisterously, she just smiled. When they quickly organized to play a game, she shrank into a corner. She was afraid she would not know what to do.

Nobody paid much attention to Katie. She was so quiet that people hardly noticed her. If they thought about it at all, they were convinced that Katie could not do anything.

The years went by. Katie grew up to be a young girl. Then she became older and older. A sickness left her a little bit crippled. She was still quiet. She was still shy, and she never seemed to do anything. She came to church regularly. She attended the Women's Mission Sewing Circle. But that is about all anybody knew about her.

One year the church Katie attended, together with the surrounding churches, decided that they would plan a relief sale so they could send more money to the Mennonite Central Committee to help the hungry and homeless people in the world. The Women's Mission Sewing Circle made a quilt for the sale. They sewed on it for weeks.

Finally the day had come. Everyone brought things they had made to the sale. There were baked goods, beautiful articles made out of wood, and many items sewn by the women's sewing circles.

The people that came to buy, went from place to place to look at the things before the auction started. They looked at the breads and pastries, they looked at the wooden chests and chairs, they looked at all the quilts. But they always stopped longest at one particular quilt. It had such a beautiful, intricate, artistic design!

"Who has made this quilt?" they asked in wonder.

The ladies standing near the quilt, smiled. "It was designed by Katie Peters," they said.

Katie was nowhere to be seen. But from that time on people knew that Katie Peters had a gift. And Katie had found a place to use her gift in the service of God and the rest of humanity.

## 90.
# *I Was In Prison*
## Around 1975

Bob Hudson was a great guy. Everybody liked him. He was a lot of fun to be with and he was friendly to all.

But Bob Hudson had one great weakness. He drank too much. He couldn't help himself. It was as if he was bound by chains. And when he drank, he didn't know what he was doing.

His wife, Ethel, started drinking, too. Then neither of them knew what they were doing.

One night Bob and Ethel came home drunk. They started arguing about some silly thing that was really of no importance, but since they had been drinking, they made a big thing of it. Bob pulled out a gun he had in his pocket. Ethel grabbed for it. He held on. They struggled. The gun went off and shot Ethel.

Now Bob was in prison. He had long since become sober. Oh, how he wished now that he had never started drinking! He had loved his wife. And now he had shot her. His friends were all gone. His relatives lived far away. All alone he sat in prison day in and day out.

No one came to see Bob Hudson. He had no one. On visiting days many of the other prisoners had friends or relatives that came to see them. But not Bob. His name was never called. It just seemed to him that he was all alone in a big ugly world that had no meaning.

One year slid by like a huge gray shadow. Then another and another. Bob did not even feel like a human being anymore since no one cared about him.

One Sunday afternoon in the springtime visitors were coming into the prison compound. Names were being called. Bob did not pay any attention to it. He just sat and sat in his cell. He did not even see the ray of sunshine peeking through the window. That too seemed something from another world which he had lost forever.

But on this Sunday afternoon, suddenly the guard called, "Bob Hudson! You have visitors."

Bob lifted his head. But immediately he dropped it again. It couldn't be. He never got visitors. He must have imagined it.

But again it came over the loudspeaker, "Bob Hudson, you have visitors!"

Slowly Bob rose to his feet. He was confused. Who could possibly have come to see him?

But it was really true. Soon he found himself sitting across from an elderly couple who said that they wanted to be his friends. Bob couldn't understand what this was all about. And when they left, he thought that was probably the last he would see of them.

But he was mistaken. The man and his wife with their friendly eyes and warm handshakes were there again the next Sunday.

Finally Bob asked them, "What's in this for you? Why do you do this? Why are you coming to see me?"

"Well," said the man, "we heard there was a man here who hadn't had any visitors for a long time. We have come to be friends with you."

That still did not make sense to Bob, but he started looking forward to the weekly visits from his new friends. Somehow the week was not so long when he knew something nice was going to happen on Sunday. Somehow the daily little indignities of prison routine were not quite so hard to bear when he knew he could tell his friends about them. And always the friendly couple brought him news of the outside world.

Bob started taking interest in life again. He appreciated the sunbeam that came into his window. He heard the birds sing. He enjoyed walking around in the prison yard. He thought about his home, his parents, his brothers and sisters again. What a lovely home they had had!

He remembered that he had gone to Sunday school when he was a boy. Slowly he recalled some of the things that were in the Bible. Suddenly he began to smile. He had remembered something that reminded him of the friendly couple who were coming to see him. It was the verse in Matthew 25: "I was in prison and you came to visit me."

He wondered about the verse. "I will ask my friends about it," he said to himself.

# 91.
# *Jamie*
## Around 1975

All night Jamie heard the sound of the rain on the roof. Not only that—he heard big rolls of thunder and sharp crackling booms. The lightning zigzagged across the sky and lit up his little room. He was frightened. He could not get up quickly because cerebral palsy had crippled his legs.

"Mother!" he called.

Just as another flash of lightning flooded the room with light, he saw his mother coming through the door.

"It is raining very hard," she said, and sat down on his bed. "I only hope the river doesn't flood."

Jamie shivered. "What if it does?" he asked. "Will the water come into our house?"

"I don't think so," said his mother. "Our house is higher up. But the people in the next block might have to get out."

The next morning at breakfast Jamie and his mother heard on the radio that the water in the river was rising higher and higher.

When his mother took Jamie to school on her way to work, the water had already covered part of the street in the next block.

In the evening Jamie and his mother stood at the edge of the water and saw boats rescuing people from the houses. There were grandmas and grandpas. There were boys and girls Jamie knew. They looked frightened.

"Where are they going?" he asked.

"They are being taken to that big church higher up," said his mother. "The Red Cross will give them some food and decide where they can sleep until they can get back to their homes."

"But their houses are full of water," cried Jamie.

"Yes, I know," said his mother. "It is going to be dreadful to clean out all the mud. I feel terri-

bly sorry for them. I wish I could help, but I have to go to work."

"I wish I could help," thought Jamie as he looked at his useless legs resting on the footrests of the wheelchair.

After several days, the water went down, but the flooded street was all muddy and there was a dreadful smell. Jamie saw old Mrs. Thompson who always smiled at him, standing in front of her house crying. He knew she was not strong enough to clean her house. And he knew she had no one to help her and nowhere to go.

That night Jamie and his mother heard over the radio that people from an organization called Mennonite Disaster Service had come from a long distance to their city to help people whose homes had been in the flood. They were shoveling out the mud and helping people fix their homes. The reporter said he had asked them why they had come, and one man had said, "We came because we want to help you. We help because this is what Jesus would want us to do."

Sure enough, the next morning, which was Saturday, Jamie saw a group of men and women and even some boys with shovels and brooms and pails get out of a big van and walk up the street. Jamie watched. Would they go to Mrs. Thompson's place? Yes, he saw two men walk into the house and start carrying out wet furniture.

Jamie was excited. He loved Jesus too. Maybe Jesus wanted him to do something. But what could he do?

Later in the day when the sun was getting hot, Jamie saw his friends Benny and John and Sara and Margaret running past his house. Soon they had a big box standing on the street corner under a tree. "What are you doing?" Jamie called when his friend Sammy rushed by too.

"We are going to sell lemonade and help the Mennonites," yelled Sammy.

"Take me too! Take me too!" called Jamie.

Sammy stopped. He looked at Jamie. "OK," he said. "You can stir the lemonade."

With Sammy pushing the wheelchair, Jamie fairly flew down the street. And the next thing he knew he was stirring the sugar in the big pitcher of lemonade. He laughed. He was glad he could help.

People came by and read the sign. "Lemonade for Sale – 5¢ a glass. Proceeds to go to Mennonite Disaster Service." The men and women smiled. The children stopped to figure out the sign and ask questions. Many bought lemonade.

At the end of the day the children had a whole dollar. When they subtracted the cost of the lemonade, they had seventy-four cents. Sammy put the money in an envelope and put a piece of paper on the lemonade stand. He wrote, "We want to give this money to Mennonite Disaster Service." Then Benny and John and Sara and Margaret and Sammy signed their names. Jamie could not write, but Sammy wrote at the bottom of the page, "Jamie Smith helped too."

Then they all brought the envelope to one of the men on the Mennonite Disaster Service team. "Thank you," said the man and smiled. "This is a real help to pay our expenses in coming here."

Jamie beamed. He had helped them to come and help Mrs. Thompson. She could live in her house again.

# 92.
# *You Owe the World Something*
## Around 1980

Margaret tried to help Sunday school teachers. One day the pastor of the Plainview Church called her and asked her to come to his church and conduct a workshop on Thursday, at 7:30 in the evening.

Margaret got everything ready. She put her books and notes and charts into her briefcase. She ate a quick supper and got into her car at 6:00. It was thirty miles to Plainview and she wanted to make sure to get to the church in good time to get everything ready for the workshop.

At first everything went well. Her old car purred along nicely as it always did and Margaret was thinking about what she was going to say to the teachers.

But, what was that? Her car slowed down. It stopped. The engine was hot. "The workshop!" thought Margaret. "How will I get to the workshop?"

It was miles from anywhere on a lonely stretch of a highway. But her car had barely rolled to a stop when Margaret saw in her rearview mirror that a truck was coming along the road.

Without thinking, she stretched her arm through the window.

The little rattling old truck passed her and then stopped. A young man got out. He came toward her and said, "What seems to be the trouble?"

Margaret did not know.

He lifted the hood and examined the motor. He shook his head. "I will tow your car to a side road," he said. "Someone will have to come and fix it."

After he had done that, he came over to Margaret and said, "Where were you going?"

"I was going to Plainview to conduct a Sunday school workshop," she said. "I am already supposed to be there."

"Well," said the man, "I will be glad to take you there, if you don't mind driving with my goldfish."

Gratefully, Margaret gathered her belongings, got out of her car and climbed up into the little truck. Sure enough, there was a huge container of something. "These must be the goldfish," she thought.

Soon they were rattling along the highway. The man was quiet.

Finally Margaret said, "I would really appreciate knowing who my good Samaritan is.

I will not tell you," said the man looking straight ahead. "That way you will not owe me, but you will owe the world something. Pass it on!"

Margaret thought about that for awhile. Then she said, "You know, the Sunday school teachers waiting for me at Plainview would not have had a workshop except for you."

"Then they owe the world something, too," remarked the man, smiling a little. "I hope they pass it on."

Margaret never found out what he was going to do with the goldfish sloshing around in the container. at her feet. He just said he liked them.

When they arrived at the church, the man asked, "Will you have someone to take you back?"

Margaret thanked him and assured him that there would be someone who would take care of her. Then she went into the church and he drove off.

For an introduction to the workshop Margaret told the teachers the story of the modern-day good Samaritan who had made it possible for her to come. "We all owe the world something," she said. "Let's pass it on."

142

# Conclusion

# 93.
# *The Light Has Come*

A long, long time ago, before Jesus went back to his heavenly Father, he told his disciples to go into all the world to tell the people everywhere about him, to bring the good news to them that God loved them and that their sins were forgiven. He told them to teach people all that he had commanded them about the way of love. He also assured them that he would send them the Holy Spirit to give them strength and courage to carry out their assignments.

Jesus kept his promise. He sent the Holy Spirit. And then the disciples all went out as Jesus had asked them to do. With great joy they told everyone that Jesus was alive, that he loved them, and that their sins were remembered no more.

The disciples started in the city of Jerusalem. They went out into the little villages of Judea. They branched out into Samaria and then went farther and farther into the world.

The Apostle Thomas went to India. Peter went to Rome. John Mark went to Egypt. Paul, the great missionary, went as far as Greece and Italy, and some think even as far as Spain.

Wherever they went, many people accepted the good news and became followers of Jesus. They in turn told others. They could not keep the good news to themselves. They wanted others to be helped as they had been helped. They wanted others to have the joy and peace they had experienced.

The good news spread farther and farther. Patrick took it to Ireland. Columba went from Ireland to Scotland. Augustine brought the good news to England. Boniface left England and went all the way to Germany.

All over Europe little bright spots appeared in the darkness of superstition and fear when the light of the good news entered people's hearts.

The time came when many, many missionaries went all over the world to spread the good news to people in India, China, Southeast Asia, Japan, Africa. The good news reached South and North America. People there told others and also went into far countries. More and more bright spots appeared in the world.

The bright spots did not increase evenly. Sometimes it took a long time until another bright spot was seen somewhere in the darkness.

Even though the good news was spreading to all countries, there were still many, many people who didn't believe it or had never heard it. There was still much darkness everywhere. People who tried to live Christ's way of love and peace were often persecuted. Many of them died for their faith. But Christ gave them strength and joy. He was with them always as he had promised.

God's great plan to turn the light on all over the world has still not been completely carried out. Every one of his followers must be a light and bring the light to others. Everyone must tell the good news in word and deed if it is to reach every person.

Jesus once said that people will come from east and west and north and south and will take their places at the feast in the kingdom of God. Jesus always keeps his promise. Some day people from all cultures and races and nations will sing praises to God together and rejoice in the love of Christ, their Savior.

# Acknowledgments

6. "A Job of His Own" (John Mark). Based on information in *Mark: The Way for All Nations* by Willard Swartley (Scottdale: Herald Press, 1979).

11. "The Gospels of Lindesfarne." Adapted from "The Gospels of Lindesfarne" in *Stories of the Book of Books* by Grace W. McGavran (New York: Friendship Press, Inc., 1947 and 1960). Used by permission.

12. "Margaret, Queen of Scotland." Based on various writings about Queen Margaret and on the author's own visit to the chapel.

13. "I Want to Read." Based on information in *Seeing Fingers: The Story of Louis Braille* by Etta DeGering (New York: David McKay Company, Inc., 1962).

14. "Who Is Guilty?" Adapted from "Eine denkwuerdige Gerichtsverhandlung" by Kong K. Kopsch, *Das Wichtigste fuer unsere Zeit*, reprinted in *Jugendblatt*, June 1, 1977.

15. "The Bible in Their Hearts." Adapted from "The Bible in Their Hearts," *Stories of the Book of Books* by Grace McGavran (New York, Friendship Press, Inc., 1947 and 1960). Used by permission.

16. "Little Tina." As told to the author by Tina's mother. The name Tina is fictitious.

18. "Too Much." From an incident related by Anne and Harold Buller, former MCC workers in Berlin.

19. "The Miracle" (Peter and Elfrieda Dyck) Based on information in *Mennonite Exodus* by Frank Epp (Altona, Manitoba: D. W. Friesen & Sons, Ltd., 1962).

20. "You Will Be Free." From *Jugendblatt* (Beilage zum *Mennoblatt*) August 1, 1977. Original source of the story is unknown.

22. "Never, Never, Never!" (Ida Scudder). Based on information in *Dr. Ida: The Story of Dr. Ida Scudder of Vellore* by Dorothy Clarke Wilson (New York: McGraw-Hill, 1959).

23. "A Christian Holy Man" (Sadhu Sundar Singh). Based on information in various writings about Sadhu Sundar Singh, especially in *Sadhu Sundar Singh Called of God* by Mrs. Arthur Parker (Old Tappan, N. J.: Fleming H. Revell, Co., 1920).

24. "He Who Loses His Life Will Save It" (Sadhu Sundar Singh). Adapted from an incident mentioned in *The Man Who Disappeared* by J. Reason (New York: Friendship Press, Inc., 1942). Used by permission.

25. "Your Hands Will Do Their Work Again" (Mary Verghese). Based on information in "From Despair to Hope," *They Lived Their Love* by Lulu Hathaway and Margaret Heppe (New York: Friendship Press, Inc., 1965). Used by permission.

26. "Where Shall We Go?" (P. A. and Elizabeth Penner). Based on information in various writings about P. A. Penner. Elizabeth Penner died in India in January, 1906. It was P. A. and Martha, his second wife, who returned to America.

27. "Your Sins Will Find You Out" (J. F. Kroeker). Based on a story related in *They Heard the Call* by Samuel T. Moyer (Newton: Faith and Life Press, 1970).

28. "That Others Might Live" (Annie Funk). Based on information in *They Heard the Call* by Samuel T. Moyer (Newton: Faith and Life Press, 1970).

29. "Who Will Help Us?" (Ezra and Elizabeth Steiner). Based on information in *With Christ on the Edge of the jungles* by Samuel T. Moyer (Jubbelpore, C. P. India: F. E. Livengood, 1941).

30. "Who Killed the Rooster?" From the experience of Dorothy and Jake Giesbrecht, missionaries to India. Used by permission.

31. "I Want to Go Back" (Annelle Wiens). From an interview with Annelle Wiens. Used with her permission.

32. "Whoever Sows Sparingly Will Reap Sparingly." Contributed by Erma Hare, India, in *Story Collection*, The Foundation Series, copyright 1978 by Evangel Press, Nappanee, Ind.; Faith and Life Press, Newton, Kans.; Mennonite Publishing House, Scottdale, Pa.

33. "An Answer to Prayer" (Hudson Taylor). Based on information in *These Sought a Country* by Kenneth Scott Latourette (New York: Harper & Brothers, 1950).

34. "Bring Them In" (Gladys Aylward). Based on information in *The Small Woman* by Alan Burgess (New York: E. P. Dutton & Co., Inc., 1957).

35. "On the Way to the Promised Land" (Gladys Aylward). Based on information in *The Small Woman* by Alan Burgess (New York: E. P. Dutton & Co., 1957).

36. "Nest-in-the-Clouds." Somewhat abbreviated from "Nest-in-den Wolken" by Winifred Waltner, printed in *Der Kinderbote*, April 1, 1957.

37. "A Great Secret" (H. J. Brown). Based on information in *Chips of Experience* by H. J. Brown, (No publisher given).

38. "All Idols Have to Go" (H. J. and Maria Brown). Adapted from *Chips of Experience* by H. J. Brown, (No publisher given).

39. "Respect for the Dead." From an interview with Marie J. Regier Janzen, former missionary to China.

40. "Do You Remember?" (Marie J. Regier). From an interview with Marie J. Regier Janzen, former missionary to China.

41. "All Power Is Given to Me." Adapted from a story by Winifred Waltner.

42. "The Call of God" (Stephen Lee). Based on a personal interview with Stephen Lee.

43. "I Forgive You" (Ann and Adoniram Judson). Based on information in *Dauntless Women* by Winifred Mathews (New York: Friendship Press, Inc., 1947). Used by permission.

44. "Why Did He Do It?" (Luke and Dorothy Beidler). From an interview with Vern Preheim, former MCC director for Asia.

45. "The Church That Grew and Grew" (Abdi Djajadihardja). From information supplied by Lois Deckert, former MCC worker in Indonesia.

46. "The Bible on the Table" (Rosella Toews). From an interview with Vern Preheim, former MCC director for Asia.

47. "The Lion and the Dove" (Vern Preheim). From an interview with Vern Preheim, former MCC director for Asia.

48. "Another Joseph" (Joseph Hardy Neesima). Based on information in *These Sought a Country* by Kenneth Scott Latourette (New York: Harper & Brothers, 1950).

49. "He Cast His Lot with the Poor" (Toyohiko Kagawa). Based on information in A *Seed Shall Serve* by Charlie May Simon (New York: E. P. Dutton & Co., Inc., 1958).

50. "The Tidal Wave." As told by Sara Harder. Original source of the story is unknown.

51. "The Shining Village." Adapted from "The Shining Village," *Stories of the Book of Books* by Grace W. McGavran (New York: Friendship Press, Inc., 1947 and 1960). Used by permission.

52. "Pray Without Ceasing." Based on a story told by Martha Janzen, missionary to Japan.

53. "What Is *Poor?*" Adapted from "The Gift" *Aiko and Her Cousin Kenichi* by Audrey McKim (New York: Friendship Press, Inc., 1967). Used by permission.

54. "We Are Ready to Go" (Masaki and Shiori Yamazaki). Based on information in an article "Japanese church sends workers to Bangladesh," *Gospel Herald*, May 26, 1981.

55. "Mother of the Taiwan Tribes Church" (Chi-o-ang). Adapted from "In the Face of Danger," *Stories of the Book of Books* by Grace W. McGavran (New York: Friendship Press, Inc., 1947 and 1960). Used by permission.

56. "A God of Love" (Mary Gau). Based on information from Sue Martens Kehler, former missionary to Taiwan.

57. "The Golden Ring." Adapted from "The Golden Ring," by Lydia Kehler, *Junior Messenger*, April 24, 1960.

58. "Opening the Way" (David and Mary Livingstone). Based on information in *Get Through or Die* by Hugh F. Frame, first published in England in 1939; (New York: Friendship Press, Inc., 1943); and *Dauntless Women* by Winifred Mathews (New York: Friendship Press, Inc., 1947). Used by permission.

59. "Singing the Bible." Adapted from "Singing the Bible," *Stories of the Book of Books* by Grace W. McGavran (New York: Friendship Press, Inc., 1947 and 1960). Used by permission.

60. "I See It Coming." Adapted from "I See It Coming" by Gertrude Jenness Rinden. From "Around the World with the Bible" in *Missionary Stories to Play and Tell* edited by Nina Millen (New York: Friendship Press, Inc., 1958). Used by permission.

61. "By the Side of the Trail." Adapted from *Missionary Stories to Play and Tell* edited by Nina Millen (New York: Friendship Press, Inc., 1958). Used by permission.

62. "Free to Fly." As told to the author by Tina Bohn, missionary in Zaire, Africa.

63. "They Could Trust Him" (Kabangu Thomas). Based on *They Didn't Use My Gun* by Pastor Kabangu Thomas (a pamphlet) and the similar story in *Footsteps to Freedom* by Levi O. Keidel where the pastor's name is "Mulumba" (Evanston, Il.: The Moody Institute, 1969).

64. "A Prepared Path" (Matthew Kazadi). Based on information in *War to Be One* by Levi O. Keidel (Grand Rapids, Mich.: The Zondervan Corporation, 1977).

65. "Famine in the Congo" (Archie Graber). Based on information in *War to Be One* by Levi O. Keidel (Grand Rapids, Mich.: The Zondervan Corporation, 1977).

66. "A Good Samaritan." From an interview with Vern Preheim, former MCC director in Algeria. The name Ahmed is fictitious.

67. "A Good Idea." From an interview with Vern Preheim.

68. "Show No Partiality." The story was told by a visitor from Africa many years ago and retold as the author remembers it.

69. "Working as a Team." Contributed by Dorothy Smoker, East Africa, in *Story Collection*, The Foundation Series, copyright 1978 by Evangel Press, Nappanee, Ind.; Faith and Life Press, Newton, Kans.; Mennonite Publishing House, Scottdale, Pa.

71. "Dayuma." Information for this story is taken from *Through Gates of Splendor* by Elizabeth Elliot (New York: Harper & Brothers, 1957), and from *Jungle Pilot, The Life and Witness of Nate Saint* by Russell T. Hitt (New York: Harper & Brothers, 1959).

72. "Dona." Adapted from an article in *Light for the Day*, 1971 by Martin Duerksen.

73. "The Search Among Thieves." Adapted from "The Search Among Thieves," *Stories of the Book of Books* by Grace W. McGavran (New York: Friendship Press, Inc., 1947 and 1960). Used by permission.

74. "Roberto and the Rabbits." As told by Reitha Klassen, former missionary to Colombia.

75. "The Importance of Every Life." From information written by Sister Susie and translated by Mariam Schmidt.

76. "Who Cares?" First written by the author for the course *Mennonite Church in Latin America* (Newton: Faith and Life Press and Scottdale: Mennonite Publishing House).

77. "We Were Strangers and They Took Us In." From an experience described by Alice Suderman.

78. "A Story of the Cheyenne." A story told by Lawrence Hart, a chief of the Cheyenne.

79. "Why Had He Failed?" From a presentation to a Social Science Seminar at Bethel College, November 1, 1978, by James Juhnke. Used with his permission.

80. "In Their Own Language" (Rodolphe Petter). Based on information in *Red Moon* by Ruth Linscheid, copyright 1973 by Ruth C. Linscheid and from *Cheyenne Trails,* by Lois Habegger (Newton, Kans.: Mennonite Publication Office, 1959).

81. "A Pulpit, an Organ and a Stove." From a conversation with the Indian leader, Ted Risingsun, at Busby, Montana, spring of 1981.

82. "A Peace Chief" (Lawrence Hart). Based on an excerpt from the commencement address by Lawrence Hart at Bethel College, Newton, Kans., May 23, 1976.

83. "He Received a Call" (Elijah McKay). From an interview with Elijah McKay, September 1981, in Winnipeg, Manitoba.

84. "A Surprise" (Elijah McKay). From an interview with Elijah McKay, September 1981, in Winnipeg, Manitoba.

85. "The Labrador Doctor" (Wilfred Grenfell). Based on information in *Forty Years for Labrador* by Sir Wilfred Grenfell (The Riverside Press, 1919 and 1932) and *Wilfred Grenfell His Life and Work* by J. Lennox Kerr (Toronto: The Ryerson Press, 1959, The Grenfell Association of Great Britain and Ireland).

86. "Hospitality" (Wilfred Grenfell). Based on information in *Forty Years for Labrador* by Sir Wilfred Grenfell (The Riverside Press, 1919 and 1932 copyright by Wilfred Grenfell).

87. "The Debt Is Paid" (David Toews). Based on information in *Mennonite Exodus* by Frank H. Epp (Altona, Manitoba: D. W. Friesen & Sons, Ltd., 1962 for Canadian Mennonite Relief and Immigration Council).

89. "I Was in Prison." An incident related by Mr. and Mrs. Albert Gaeddert about a couple in the prison ministry. The name Bob Hudson is fictitious.

91. "Jamie." The incident is taken from *Day of Disaster* by Katie Funk Wiebe (Scottdale, Pa.: Herald Press, 1976).